Peter Bilhorn

Crowning glory No. 2

A choice collection of gospel hymns

Peter Bilhorn

Crowning glory No. 2
A choice collection of gospel hymns

ISBN/EAN: 9783337269609

Printed in Europe, USA, Canada, Australia, Japan

Cover: Foto ©Andreas Hilbeck / pixelio.de

More available books at **www.hansebooks.com**

CROWNING GLORY

No. 2.

A COLLECTION OF

Gospel Hymns

—— BY ——

PETER BILHORN.

—— PUBLISHED BY ——

148 Madison St. **P. BILHORN,** Chicago, Ill.

Y. M. C. A., Fifth Floor.

PRICE BY MAIL 35C PER COPY.   BY EXPRESS, NOT PREPAID, $3.60 PER DOZEN. $30.00 PER HUNDRED.

Preface.

May the FATHER, SON, and the HOLY SPIRIT add their blessing to this collection of songs, even more than that of No. 1. We believe, if these hymns are sung according to I Cor. 14:15, that they will wing their way to open and melt the hard and stony heart of the unbeliever, and cause the Christian believer to rejoice in the LORD, Who saves a poor sinner like me.

Yours, in the Gospel Bonds,

"Till HE Come,"

THE PUBLISHER.

NOTE—The No. 2 collection is entirely separate from No. 1, excepting the words only of three old hymns, viz.: "All Hail the Power of Jesus' Name," "Just as I am," and "Come, Every Soul by Sin Oppressed."

ANDERSON BROS., MUSIC TYPOGRAPHERS, 354 DEARBORN ST., CHICAGO, ILL.

Printed and Bound by
W. U. CONKEY COMPANY, Chicago.

CROWNING GLORY.

❧NO. 2.❧

No. 1. **Blest Three in One.**

P. B. P. BILHORN.

1. Praise to the Fa - ther, blest be the Son, Wel - come the
2. Loved by the Fa - ther, saved by the Son, Sealed by the
3. O bless - ed Spir - it, come now with - in, Burn up each
4. He that be - liev - eth on God's own Son, Hath in him

spir - it, blest Three in One; God planned re - demp - tion,
spir - it, blest Three in One; Cleansed by Thy wash - ing,
i - dol, cleanse us from sin; Great God our Fa - ther,
wit - ness, life has be - gun; Spir - it doth wit - ness,

Christ free - ly came, Spir - it doth quick-en these three the same.
filled would I be, Thee now to hon - or, blest Trin - i - ty.
Thy will be done, Je - sus our Broth-er, blest Three in One.
word lead - eth on, Blood dai - ly cleans-eth, blest Three in One.

Copyright, 1891, by P. Bilhorn.

No. 2.   Jesus Saves.

PRISCILLA J. OWENS.　　　　　　　　　　　　WM. J. KIRPATRICK. By per.

1. We have heard a joy - ful sound, Je - sus saves, Je - sus saves;
2. Waft it on the roll - ing tide, Je - sus saves, Je - sus saves;
3. Sing a - bove the bat - tle's strife, Je - sus saves, Je - sus saves;
4. Give the winds a might - y voice, Je - sus saves, Je - sus saves;

Spread the glad - ness all a - round, Je - sus saves, Je - sus saves;
Tell to sin - ners, far and wide, Je - sus saves, Je - sus saves;
By His death and end - less life, Je - sus saves, Je - sus saves;
Let the na - tions now re - joice, Je - sus saves, Je - sus saves;

Bear the news to ev - 'ry land, Climb the steeps and cross the waves,
Sing, ye is - lands of the sea, Ech - o back, ye o - cean caves,
Sing it soft - ly thro' the gloom, When the heart for mer - cy craves,
Shout sal - va - tion full and free, High - est hills and deep - est caves,

On - ward, 'tis our Lord's com - mand, Je - sus saves, Je - sus saves.
Earth shall keep her Ju - bi - lee, Je - sus saves, Je - sus saves.
Sing in tri - umph o'er the tomb, Je - sus saves, Je - sus saves.
This our song of vic - to - ry, Je - sus saves, Je - sus saves.

No. 3. Risen with Him.

Col. 3:1.

Miss JULIA H. JOHNSTON.   P. BILHORN.

1. Hear the an-gel's glo-rious mes-sage Break-ing thro' the night of gloom,
2. Saints be-low, thro' Him tri-um-phant, Following where His feet have trod;
3. Ye who share His res-ur rec-tion, Raised to life thro' sec-ond birth,
4. Dead to sin, with Je-sus ris-en, Walk in Him, in love and fear,

Fear ye not! the Lord is ris-en, Lo! the emp-ty tomb.
Is your life and all your treas-ure, Hid with Christ in God?
Set on Him your heart's af-fec-tion, Not on things of earth.
When He shall ap-pear in glo-ry, Then shall ye ap-pear.

CHORUS.

Ris-en Lord! as-cend-ed Sav-ior! He is throned in light and love;

If ye then with Him be ris-en, Seek those things a-bove.

The Beloved.

H. M. BRADLEY.   THOS. O. LOWE.

1. Down in the val - ley, a - mong the sweet lil - ies,
2. Know'st Thou I seek Thee? oh, haste to dis - cov - er
3. Now I ap - proach Thee, oh, fair - est Re - deem - er,
4. Gen - tler Thy voice than the whis - per of an - gels,

Walks my Be - lov - ed, His foot - prints I see; Haste I to
Where is the place of Thy fra - grant re - treat—Where Thou dost
Lured by Thy beau - ty to dwell in Thy love; Hide not Thy
Bright - er Thy smile than the sun in the sky; Gath - er me

fol - low Thee, Sav - ior and Lov - er, How the winds whis - per Thy
rest with Thy flocks at the noon - tide, Shel - ter'd near fount - ains un-
face from the heart that a - dores Thee, Hast Thou not sought me and
ten - der - ly, close to Thy bo - som, Faint with Thy lov - li - ness

CHORUS.

dear name to me! }
search'd by the heat? }
called me Thy Dove? } Oh, my be - lov - ed Lord! For me Thy
thus let me die. }

life - blood pour'd, Thou bless - ed Son of God, Je - sus, my Lord.

By permission.

No. 5. Where the Living Waters Flow.

Words arr.

EDWARD E. NICKERSON.

1. Rest to the wea-ry soul And ach-ing breast is giv'n, Down where the
2. For thee, my soul, for thee These priceless joys were bought, Down where the
3. Come, with the ransom'd train, The Sav-ior's prais-es sing. Down where the
4. And soon, be-fore His face, We'll praise in light a-bove. Down where the

liv-ing waters flow; Grace makes the wound-ed whole, Love fills our heart with heav'n,
liv-ing waters flow; Thine is the mer-cy free That Christ to earth has brought,
liv-ing waters flow; Rejoice! the Lamb was slain. A-dore! He reigns a King,
liv-ing waters flow; Tri-umph-ant thro' His grace, Made per-fect by His love,

REFRAIN.

Down where the living waters flow. Down where the living waters flow, ...
living waters flow,

Down where the tree of life doth grow, I'm liv-ing in the light, for

Je-sus and the right, Down where the liv-ing waters flow.
living wa-ters flow.

No. 6. Farewell.

W. P. FIFE. P. BILHORN.

1. How swift-ly the years of our pil-grim-age fly, As weeks, months and
2. The right-eous and wick-ed move swift-ly a-long, In crowds to the
3. To you, fel-low Christ-ians, I turn with de-light, The grave can not
4. Fare-well, fel-low sin-ners, I'm free from your blood, My mes-sage de-

sea-sons roll si-lent-ly by; Our days are soon numbered, and
grave, both the old and the young; The good rise to heav-en, the
harm you, your fu-ture is bright; Be faith-ful and hum-ble, temp-
liv-ered, I leave you with God; I've begged and per-suad-ed, but

Rit.

death sounds our knell, We scarce know our friends till we bid them fare-well.
bad sink to hell, They take on life's verge an e-ter-nal fare-well.
ta-tions re-pel, You'll soon leave this world with a smil-ing fare-well.
can not com-pel; Till judg-ment day there-fore, I bid you fare-well.

CHO.—Fare-well, ... fare-well, ...

I'll bid you farewell, I'll bid you farewell, I've begged and per-suad-ed, but can not compel;

Fare-well, ... fare-well, ...

Rit.

I'll bid you farewell, I'll bid you farewell, Till judgment day therefore, I'll bid you farewell.

No. 7 God be Merciful to Me.

Ps. 51.

P. B.

P. BILHORN.

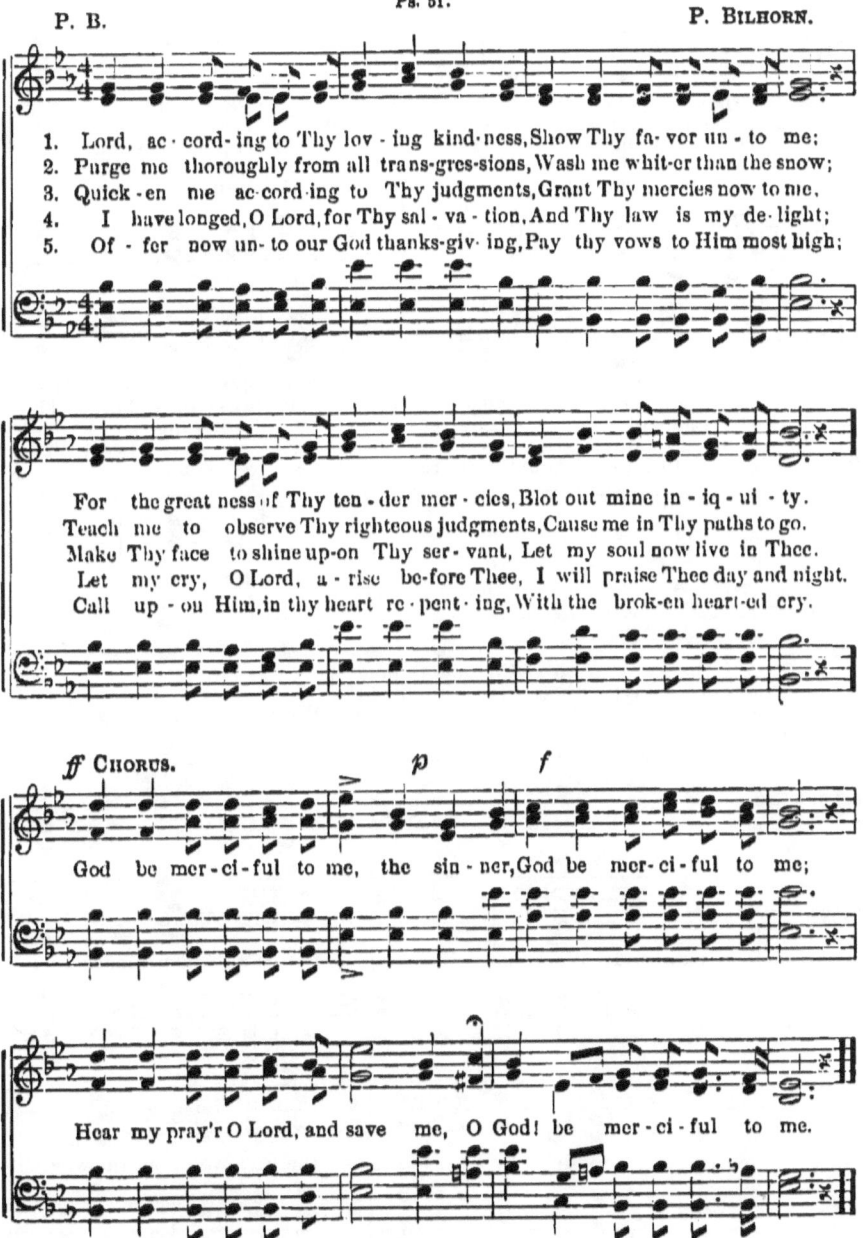

1. Lord, ac·cord·ing to Thy lov·ing kind·ness, Show Thy fa·vor un·to me;
2. Purge me thoroughly from all trans·gres·sions, Wash me whit·er than the snow;
3. Quick·en me ac·cord·ing to Thy judgments, Grant Thy mercies now to me,
4. I have longed, O Lord, for Thy sal·va·tion, And Thy law is my de·light;
5. Of·fer now un·to our God thanks·giv·ing, Pay thy vows to Him most high;

For the great·ness of Thy ten·der mer·cies, Blot out mine in·iq·ui·ty.
Teach me to observe Thy righteous judgments, Cause me in Thy paths to go.
Make Thy face to shine up·on Thy ser·vant, Let my soul now live in Thee.
Let my cry, O Lord, a·rise be·fore Thee, I will praise Thee day and night.
Call up·on Him, in thy heart re·pent·ing, With the brok·en heart·ed cry.

ff CHORUS.

God be mer·ci·ful to me, the sin·ner, God be mer·ci·ful to me;

Hear my pray'r O Lord, and save me, O God! be mer·ci·ful to me.

No. 8. We're on the way to Canaan's Land.

Rev. H. G. Jackson.

W. S. Nickle.

1. From E-gypt's cru - el bond - age fled, O - be - dient to our
2. Thro' wil - der - ness - es wide and drear, Our Lord will guide our
3. His pow'r the smit - ten rock con - trols, A crys - tal stream our
4. In hos - tile lands we feel no fear; No foe our on - ward
5. Ere long, the riv - er cross'd, we'll meet The ran - somed host at

Lord's com-mand, And by His word and spir - it led, We're
steps a - right, Be - hold to prove His pres - ence here, The
need sup - plies, He feeds our hun - gry, faint - ing souls, With
march can stay; In ev - 'ry con - flict He is near, Whose
His right hand; And there re - ceive a wel - come sweet, From

CHORUS.

on the way to Ca - naan's land!
cloud by day, the fire by night!
dai - ly man - na from the skies! We're on the way, a
pres - ence cheers us on the way.
our dear Lord to Ca - naan's land!

pil - grim band; We're on the way to Ca - naan's land; Di -

vine - ly guid - ed day by day, We're on the way, we're on the way.

No. 9.

Only a Touch!

Mark 5. 25-34.

Mrs Cynthie H. Wilson.

P. Bilhorn.

Not too fast.

1 On - ly a touch of the trem - u - lous hand, As the
2 On - ly a touch! but the an - swer came swift, And tho'
3 On - ly a touch of the trem - u - lous soul, As she
4. On - ly a touch of His gar - ment's hem, With a

cu - ri - ous throng drew nigh; On - ly a touch! but how
all of her liv - ing was spent, On - ly a touch! what a
pressed in the surg - ing throng; On - ly a touch! yet it
hope in His heal - ing grace; On - ly a touch! with a

won - drous and grand! The Mas - ter was pass - ing by
glo - ri - ous gift, The heal - ing to her was sent.
made her whole, And vir - tue had made her strong
faith in Him, He turned and be - held her face.

Refrain. *cres.*

On - ly a touch! on - ly a touch! Touch Him and you'll know why;

rit.

On - ly a touch of His garment's hem, O touch Him! ere He pass by.

No. 10. Gathering Home.

MARY LESLIE.

W. A. OGDEN.

1. They're gathering homeward from ev - 'ry land, One by one! one by one!
2. We too must come to the riv - er - side, One by one! one by one!
3. Jesus, Re - deem - er, we look to Thee, One by one! one by one!

As their wea-ry feet touch the shin-ing strand, Yes, one by one!
We are near-er its wa - ters each e - ven-tide, Yes, one by one!
We lift up our voi - ces trembling-ly, Yes, one by one!

They rest with the Sav - ior, they wait their crown, Their trav-el-stained
We can hear the noise and the dash-ing stream, Oft now and a-
The waves of the riv - er are dark and cold, We know not the

gar - ments are all laid down; They wait the white rai - ment the
gain, thro' our life's deep dream; Some-times the dark floods all the
place where our feet may hold; O Thou who didst pass thro' the

Lord shall pre-pare, For all who the glo - ry with Him shall share.
banks o - ver-flow, Some - times in rip - ples and small waves go.
deep - est mid-night, Now guide us, and send us the staff of light.

By permission.

Gathering Home. Concluded.

REFRAIN.

Gath'ring home! gath'ring home! Ford-ing the riv-er one by one!

Gath-'ring home! gath-'ring home, yes, one by one!

No. 11. Something Jesus Gave Me.

GRACE WEBSTER HINSDALE.   Rev. ALFRED TAYLOR. By per.

1. I have some-thing Je - sus gave me for my own; It is
2. In its - self it hath no val - ue more than tears; Tho' I'm
3. Like His pres-ence it doth bring me peace di - vine; 'Tis His
4. If my hu - man hands had found it, I should grieve; But my

some-thing which He sent me from His throne; It is some-thing which I
wea - ry as I bear it, I've no fears; It is pre-cious as a
sweet and ten - der whis-per, Thou art mine. What's the gift I clasp so
Je - sus laid it on me, I be - lieve. Oh, how sweet it is to

car - ry near my heart: It is safe till Je - sus bids me from it part.
to - ken from the Lord. That His heart-tho't is as lov-ing as His word.
close-ly wouldst thou see? 'Tis a cross which Christ, my Mas-ter sent, to me.
bear it as His gift! While the bur - den of my treasure Christ doth lift.

No. 12. Sunshine in the Soul.

E. E. Hewitt.

Jno. R. Sweney. By per.

1. There's sun-shine in my soul to-day, More glo-ri-ous and bright
2. There's mu-sic in my soul to-day, A car-ol to my King,
3. There's spring-time in my soul to-day, For when the Lord is near,
4. There's glad-ness in my soul to-day, And hope, and praise, and love,

Than grows in an-y earth-ly sky, For Je-sus is my light.
And Je-sus, list-en-ing, can hear The song I can-not sing.
The dove of peace sings in my heart, The flow'rs of grace ap-pear.
For bless-ings which He gives me now, For joys "laid up" a-bove.

REFRAIN.

Oh, there's sun — — shine, Bless-ed sun — — shine,
Oh, there's sun-shine in the soul, Bless-ed sun-shine in the soul,

While the peace-ful, hap-py mo-ments roll; When
hap-py mo-ments roll,

Je-sus shows His smil-ing face There is sun-shine in the soul.

No. 13.

Come Near Me.

G. W. L.

J. W. B.

Tenderly.

1. Come near me, O my Sav-ior; Thy ten-der-ness re-veal; O,
2. Come near me, my Re-deem-er, And nev-er leave my side; My
3. Come near me, bless-ed Je-sus, I need Thee in my joy, No
4. Be near me, might-y Sav-ior, When comes the lat-est strife; For

let me know the sym-pa-thy Which Thou for me dost feel. I
bark, when toss'd on troub-le's sea, The storm can-not out-ride, Un-
less than when the dir-est ills My hap-pi-ness de-stroy; For
Thou hast thro' death's shad-ows pass'd, And ope'd the gates of life: And

f   *mf*

need Thee ev-'ry mo-ment; Thine ab-sence brings dis-may; But
less Thy word of pow-er Ar-rest the surg-ing wave, No
when the sun shines o'er me, And flow-ers strew my way, With-
when a-mong the ran-som'd I stand with crown and palm, To

Cres.   *Dim.*

when the tempt-er hurls his darts, 'Twere death with Thee a-way.
voice but Thine its rage can quell, No arm but Thine can save.
out Thy wise and guid-ing hand More eas-i-ly I stray.
Thee, Di-vine, un-fail-ing Friend, I'll raise th' e-ter-nal psalm.

By permission.

No. 14. Glory, O Glory!

Miss Ada Blenkhorn.   P. Bilhorn.

1. I found in Christ a Savior, To save me ev-'ry day,
2. He gives me sweet-est com-forts, He ev-'ry sor-row shares,
3. He leads me forth to bat-tle, He is my shield and sword,
4. He is my might-y Lead-er, He is the great "I Am,"

He fills me with His pres-ence, He leads me all the way.
And while be-low I tar-ry, My man-sion He pre-pares.
And to my trust-ing spir-it, Ex-ceed-ing great re-ward.
I shall, in ev-'ry con-flict, Be vic-tor through the Lamb.

Chorus.

O glo-ry, O glo-ry!
My soul is filled with glo-ry! To Him my voice I'll raise;

O glo-ry, O glo-ry!
O glo-ry, to Him glo-ry! His name I'll ev-er praise.

No. 15. Redeemed, Praise the Lord

Abbie Mills.

Wm. J. Kirkpatrick.

1. O hap-py day! what a Sav-ior is mine! I am redeemed, praise the Lord!
2. O clap your hands, all ye peo-ple of God, I am redeemed, praise the Lord!
3. Thanks be to God for the great vict'ry given, I am redeemed, praise the Lord!
4. Glo-ry to God, I would shout ev-er-more, I am redeemed, praise the Lord!

Fine.

All to His pleas-ure I glad-ly re-sign, I am redeemed, praise the Lord!
Let ev-'ry tongue speak His mer-cy a-broad, I am redeemed, praise the Lord!
Now I am free, ev-'ry chain has been riven, I am redeemed, praise the Lord!
O for a voice that could reach ev-'ry shore, I am redeemed, praise the Lord!

Je-sus has tak-en my bur-den a-way; Je-sus has turn'd all my night in-to day;
His loving kindness is better than gold; He doth bestow more than my cup can hold;
Out of the pit, and the mire, and the clay, Je-sus has borne me in triumph away;
Help me, ye ransom'd, awake, ev'ry string, Let earth rejoice and the whole heav-ens ring,

Use first four lines as Chorus. D.C.

Je-sus has come to my heart, come to stay, I am redeemed, praise the Lord!
Wondrous sal vation, that ne'er can be told, I am redeemed, praise the Lord!
Safe on the Rock I am stand-ing to-day, I am redeemed, praise the Lord!
While we the cho-rus u-ni-ted-ly sing, I am redeemed, praise the Lord!

No. 16. When Jesus Came Our Way.

An Experience Meeting at Capernaum.

Rev. H. B. TOWNSEND.　　　　　　　　　　　　　　　　P. BILHORN.

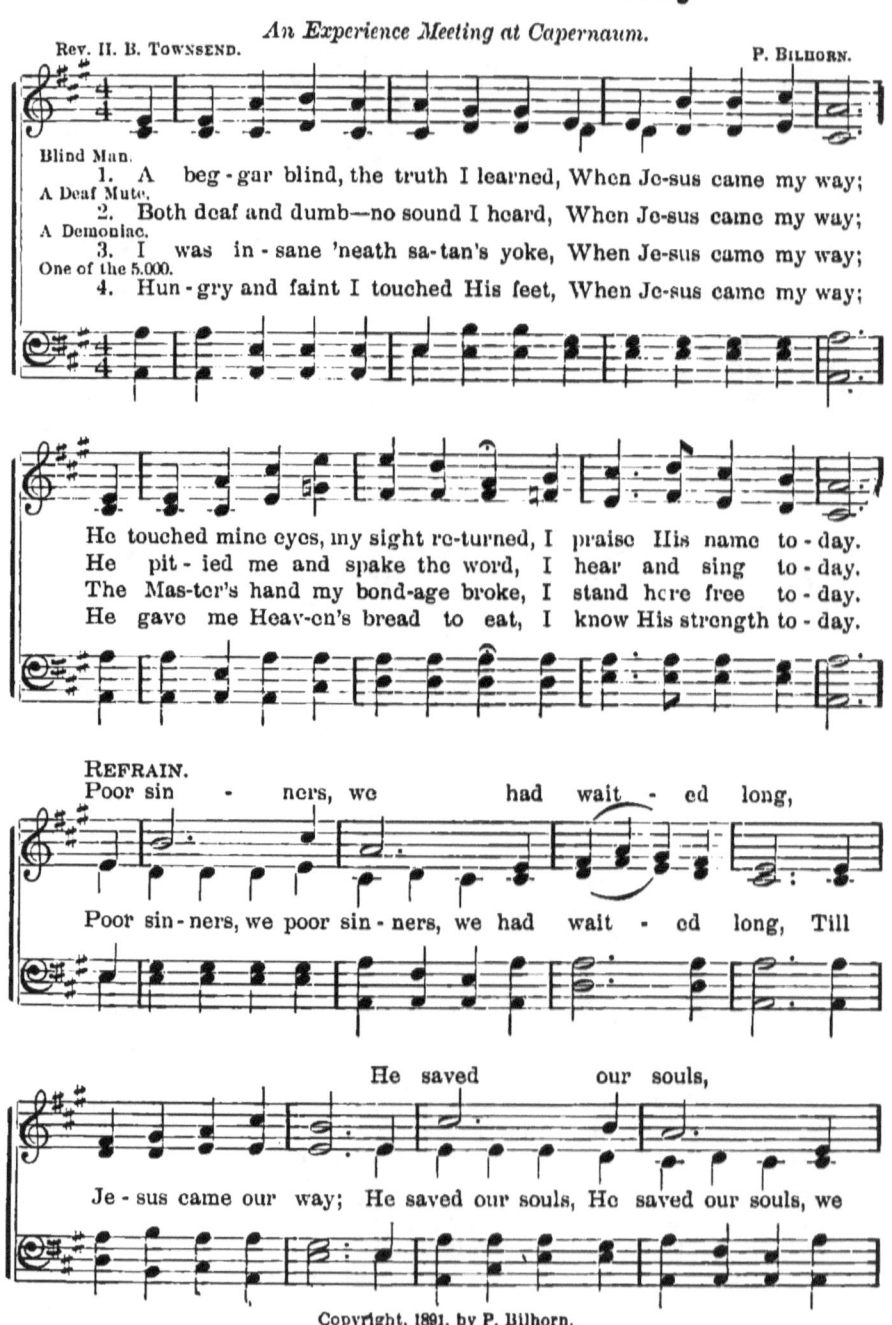

Blind Man.
1. A beg-gar blind, the truth I learned, When Je-sus came my way;
A Deaf Mute.
2. Both deaf and dumb—no sound I heard, When Je-sus came my way;
A Demoniac.
3. I was in-sane 'neath sa-tan's yoke, When Je-sus came my way;
One of the 5,000.
4. Hun-gry and faint I touched His feet, When Je-sus came my way;

He touched mine eyes, my sight re-turned, I praise His name to-day.
He pit-ied me and spake the word, I hear and sing to-day.
The Mas-ter's hand my bond-age broke, I stand here free to-day.
He gave me Heav-en's bread to eat, I know His strength to-day.

REFRAIN.

Poor sin - ners, we had wait - ed long,

Poor sin-ners, we poor sin-ners, we had wait - ed long, Till

He saved our souls,

Je - sus came our way; He saved our souls, He saved our souls, we

When Jesus Came Our Way. Concluded.

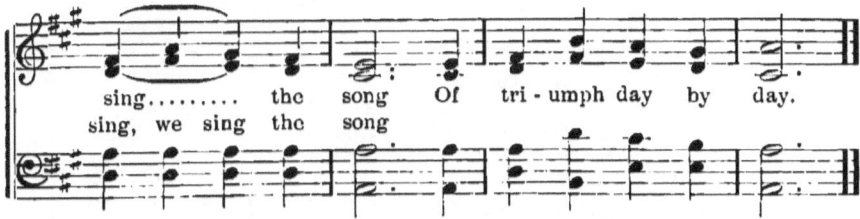

sing........ the song Of tri-umph day by day.
sing, we sing the song

The Paralytic.
5 With palsy I was trembling long,
   When Jesus came my way,
   He found me weak, He made me strong,
   I, too, rejoice to-day.

A Leper.
6 A leprous man—outcast and sad,
   When Jesus came my way;
   He gave me health and made me glad,
   I'm cleansed from sin to-day.

Widow's Son from Nain.
7 A dead son I was borne by men,
   When Jesus came my way;
   He stopped the bier, I live again,
   I now His will obey.

All.
8 We all were lost in sin and shame,
   When Jesus came our way;
   He saved us! Bless His holy name,
   His word we now obey.

No. 17. My Faith Looks up to Thee.

RAY PALMER.   LOWELL MASON.

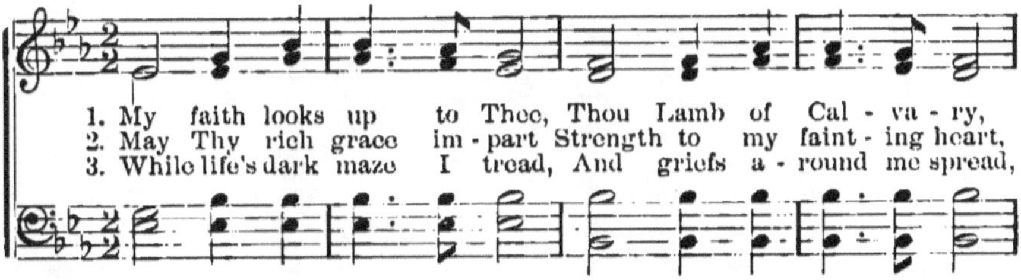

1. My faith looks up to Thee, Thou Lamb of Cal-va-ry,
2. May Thy rich grace im-part Strength to my faint-ing heart,
3. While life's dark maze I tread, And griefs a-round me spread,

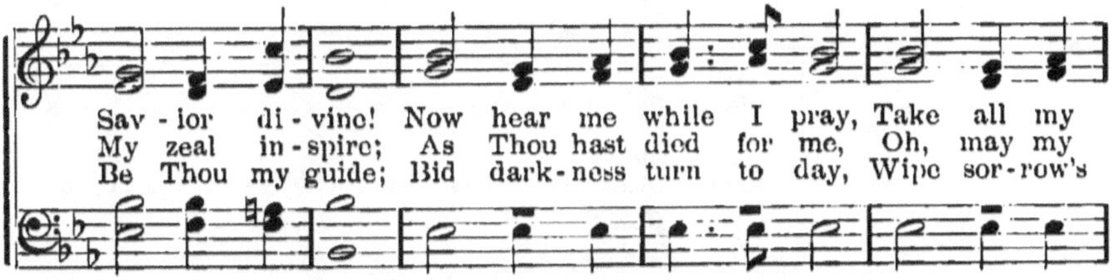

Sav-ior di-vine! Now hear me while I pray, Take all my
My zeal in-spire; As Thou hast died for me, Oh, may my
Be Thou my guide; Bid dark-ness turn to day, Wipe sor-row's

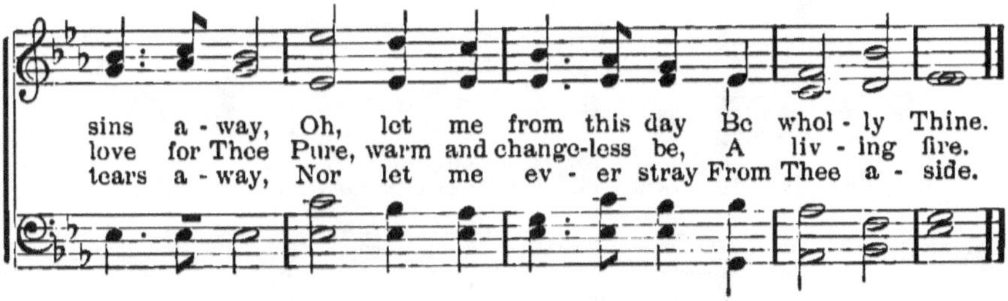

sins a-way, Oh, let me from this day Be whol-ly Thine.
love for Thee Pure, warm and change-less be, A liv-ing fire.
tears a-way, Nor let me ev-er stray From Thee a-side.

No. 18. The Savior Precious.

JAMES S. APPLE.   JNO. R. SWENEY.

1. I have found the Sav-ior precious, And I love Him more and more;
   I have found the Sav-ior precious, And I find Him pre-cious still;
2. I have found the Sav-ior precious, And wher-ev-er I may go,
   I am read-y, if He calls me, In the bat-tle field to stand;

He has rolled a-way my bur-den, And my mourning days are o'er;
All my life is con-se-cra-ted To His (*Omit.*)
I will bear the roy-al stan-dard, And its col-ors I will show;
I am read-y—yes, and wait-ing—To ful- (*Omit.*)

CHORUS.

ser-vice and His will. I have tak - - - en up the
fill my Lord's command. I have tak-en up the cross, And will

cross, And will nev - - - er lay it
nev-er lay it down, I have tak-en up the cross, And will

down Till I see................ His face in
nev-er lay it down Till I see His face in glo-ry, Till I

The Savior Precious. Concluded.

glo - ry, And re-ceive........... a star - ry crown.
see His face in glo-ry, And re-ceive a star-ry crown, a star - ry crown.

3 I have found the Savior precious;
  Hallelujah! praise His name!
To a mansion in His kingdom
  Thro' His grace the right I claim.

I have found the Savior precious;
  He has proved my dearest Friend;
And my faith can trust His promise
  Of protection to the end.

No. 19. What a Friend.

H. BONAR.　　　　　　　　　　　　C. C. CONVERSE. By per.

1. What a friend we have in Je - sus, All our sins and griefs to bear?

S.

FINE.

What a priv - i - lege to car - ry Ev - 'ry thing to God in prayer.
D. S. All be-cause we do not car - ry Ev - 'ry thing to God in prayer.

D. S.

Oh, what peace we oft - en for - feit, Oh, what need-less pain we bear,

2 Have we trials and temptations?
  Is there trouble anywhere?
We should never be discouraged,
  Take it to the Lord in prayer.
Can we find a friend so faithful,
  Who will all our sorrows share?
Jesus knows our every weakness,
  Take it to the Lord in prayer.

3 Are we weak and heavy-laden,
  Cumbered with a load of care?
Precious Savior, still our refuge,—
  Take it to the Lord in prayer.
Do thy friends despise, forsake thee?
  Take it to the Lord in prayer;
In His arms he'll take and shield thee,
  Thou wilt find a solace there.

No. 20.   Bid Him Come In.

P. B.   P. Bilhorn.

1. Oh, what a Sav - ior, He's plead-ing for you, Plead-ing for you,
2. Will you not trust Him as Sav - ior to - day? Trust Him to - day?
3. O - pen your heart's door and bid Him come in? Bid Him come in,
4. Come now to Je - sus, for why will you die? Why will you die?

plead-ing for you; Come and ac - cept Him, He's lov - ing and true,
trust Him to - day? He will drive sor - row and sigh-ing a - way,
bid Him come in; He hath re-deemed you, He'll cleanse you from sin,
why will you die? While He in mer - cy is com-ing so nigh,

CHORUS.

'Tis Je - sus now plead-ing for you.   Shall.......... He come
Will you not trust Je - sus to - day?
Oh, bid the dear Sav - ior come in.
Oh, broth - er, then why will you die?   Shall He come in?

in?........ Shall....... He come in?........ Will.......
Shall He come in? He will re-deem you and save you from sin; Bid Him come in,

Bid Him Come In. Concluded.

you not bid............ the dear Sav - - ior come in?
bid Him come in, Bid the dear Sav-ior come in.

No. 21. Art Thou Drifting?

P. B. P. BILHORN.

1. Oh! my broth-er, art thou drift-ing? Drift-ing tow'rd a sea?
2. At its mouth lie rocks tre-men-dous, Black-er than de-spair,
3. Hark! the wild white waves are foam-ing, Hun-gry, fierce and bold,
4. But be-yond those rag-ing bil-lows, Lies a hap-py shore,
5. Oh! my friend, thy bark shall nev-er Reach that hap-py shore,
6. Call Him with en-treat-y ur-gent, Call Him near thy side,

From whose shore no bark re-turn-eth, 'Tis E-ter-ni-ty.
Many a no-ble bark, my broth-er, Has been shipwreck'd there.
O'er the shattered ves-sel dash-ing, Dread-ful, i-cy, cold.
Where the saints redeemed thro' Je-sus, Dwell for ev-er-more.
Till the Lord be-comes your Pi-lot: He will guide thee o'er.
Then o'er rough-est, dark-est bil-lows, Safe-ly thou shalt glide.

CHORUS.

Oh! my broth-er, art thou drift-ing, Drift-ing to e-ter-ni-ty?

Copyright, 1891, by P. Bilhorn.

No. 22. Hiding in the Rock.

Rev. H. B. Hartzler.   Chas. H. Gabriel. By per.

1. In the Rock of A - ges hid - ing, I have found a sure re-
2. In the Rock of A - ges rest - ing, I en - joy a sweet re-
3. In the Rock of A - ges trust - ing, I am kept in per - fect

treat; In the Ref - uge now a - bid - ing, I have found a joy com-plete.
pose, Where the grace of God for - ev - er Like a might - y riv - er flows.
peace; In the hope of glo - ry wait - ing, Till the toil of life shall cease.

CHORUS.

While the storm a - round me rag - es, And the an - gry bil - lows roar,

I am hid-ing in the Rock of A - ges, I am safe for ev - er - more.

No. 23. Jesus Will Give You Rest.

FANNY J. CROSBY.   JNO. R. SWENEY. By per.

1. Will you come, will you come, with your poor, bro-ken heart, Burden'd with
2. Will you come, will you come? there is mer-cy for you, Balm for your
3. Will you come, will you come? you have noth-ing to pay; Je-sus, who
4. Will you come, will you come? how He pleads with you now! Fly to His

sin op-press'd? Lay it down at the feet of your Sav-ior and Lord,
ach-ing breast; On-ly come as you are, and be-lieve on His name,
loves you best, By His death on the Cross pur-chas'd life for your soul,
lov-ing breast, And what-ev-er your sin or your sor-row may be,

REFRAIN.

Je-sus will give you rest.   Oh, hap-py rest, sweet, hap-py rest!

Je-sus will give you rest,(hap-py rest,) Oh! why won't you come in

sim-ple, trust-ing faith? Je-sus will give you rest.

No. 24. A Little Talk with Jesus.

P. BILHORN.

1. Just a lit-tle talk with Je-sus, How it smooths the rug-ged road!
2. Ah, this is what I'm want-ing, His love-ly face to see;
3. I can-not live with-out Him, Nor would I if I could;
4. So I'll wait a lit-tle long-er, Till His ap-point-ed time,

How it seems to help me on-ward, When I faint be-neath my load;
And I'm not a-fraid to say it, I know He's want-ing me.
He is my dai-ly por-tion, My com-fort-er and food.
And a-long the up-ward path-way, My pil-grim feet shall climb.

When my heart is crushed with sor-row, And my eyes with tears are dim,
He gave His life a ran-som, To make me all His own,
He is al-to-geth-er love-ly; None can with Him com-pare;
There, in my Fa-ther's dwelling, Where ma-ny man-sions be,

There is naught can yield me com-fort Like a lit-tle talk with Him.
And He'll ne'er for-get His prom-ise To me, His purchased one.
The chief-est of ten thou-sand, And fair-est of the fair.
I shall sweet-ly talk with Je-sus, And He will talk with me.

A Little Talk with Jesus. Concluded.

REFRAIN.

A lit - tle talk with Him, A lit - tle talk with Him,

There's naught can yield me com - fort Like a lit - tle talk with Him.

No. 25.   Enough for Me.

E. A. H.

Rev. F. A. Hoffman. By per.

1. O love sur-pass-ing knowl-edge! O grace so full and free!
2. O won-der-ful sal - va-tion! From sin He makes me free!
3. O blood of Christ, so pre-cious, Poured out on Cal - va - ry!

FINE.

I know that Je - sus saves me, And that's e-nough for me.
I feel the sweet as - sur-ance, And that's e-nough for me.
I feel its cleans-ing pow - er, And that's e-nough for me.

D. S. *I know that Je - sus saves me, And that's e-nough for me!*

REFRAIN.

D. S.

And that's e-nough for me! And that's e-nough for me!

No. 26.   There is Life for a Look.

AMELIA M. HULL.   Isa. 45: 22.   E. C. AVIS.

1. There is life for a look at the cru - ci - fied One, There is
2. Oh, why was He there as the Bear - er of sin, If on
3. It is not thy tears of re - pent-ance and prayers, But the
4. Then take, with re - joic-ing, from Je - sus at once, The

life at this mo-ment for thee; Then look, sin - ner, look un - to
Je - sus thy guilt was not laid? Oh, why from His side flowed the
blood that a - tones for the soul; On Him, then, who shed it, thou
life ev - er - last-ing He gives, And know with as - sur-ance thou

Him and be saved, Un - to Him who was nailed to the tree.
sin - cleans-ing blood, If His dy - ing thy debt has not paid?
may - est, at once, Thy weight of in - i - qui - ties roll.
nev - er canst die, Since Je - sus thy right-eous-ness lives.

REFRAIN.

Then look   un - to Him,   Then look unto Him and be saved, (and be saved);
sinner, look,   and be sav'd,

There is life for a look at the crucified One, There is life at this moment for thee.

Copyright, 1887, by E. C. Avis. By per.

No. 27.   Onward, Christian Soldiers!

GOULD.   SULLIVAN.

1. On-ward, Christian sol - diers! Marching as to war, With the cross of
2. Like a might-y arm - y Moves the Church of God; Brothers, we are
3. Crowns and thrones may per-ish, Kingdoms rise and wane, But the Church of
4. Onward, then, ye peo - ple! Join our hap - py throng, Blend with ours your

Je - sus Go - ing on be - fore. Christ, the roy - al Mas - ter,
tread-ing Where the saints have trod; We are not di - vid - ed,
Je - sus Con-stant will re - main; Gates of hell can nev - er
voi - ces In the tri - umph-song; Glo - ry, laud, and hon - or

Leads a - gainst the foe; For-ward in - to bat - tle, See, His ban - ners
All one bod - y we; One in hope and doc-trine, One in char - i -
'Gainst that Church prevail; We have Christ's own promise, And that can not
Un - to Christ, the King, This thro' countless a - ges Men and an - gels

go!
ty.
fail. } On-ward, Christian sol - diers! Marching as to war,
sing.

With the Cross of Je - sus Go - ing on be - fore.

No. 28. The Home without a Sorrow.

P. B.

P. BILHORN.

1. There's a home be-yond this vale of tears, Where we'll
2. Far be-yond the bonds of grief and pain, We will
3. What a joy-ous tho't now fills my heart, For we'll
4. Then re-joice, ye ran-somed of the Lord, We will

nev-er know a sor-row or a care; 'Tis be-yond this life of
nev-er know a sor-row or a care; All the lov'd ones gone we'll
nev-er know a sor-row when we're there; And from friends and kindred
nev-er know a sor-row or a care; 'Tis re-cord-ed in His

toil and fears, We will nev-er know a sor-row when we're there.
meet a-gain, And we'll nev-er know a sor-row when we're there.
nev-er part, We will nev-er know a sor-row or a care.
bless-ed word, That we'll nev-er know a sor-row when we're there.

CHORUS.

When we're there, o-ver there, We will
When we're there, o-ver there,

The Home without a Sorrow. Concluded.

nev-er know a sor-row or a care, When we're there,
o-ver there, When we're there,

o-ver there, We will nev-er know a sor-row o-ver there.
o-ver there,

Rit.

No. 29. Guide Me.

Rev. W. Williams. Wm. L. Viner.

FINE.

1. Guide me, O Thou great Je-ho-vah! Pil-grim thro' this bar-ren land:
D. C. Bread of heav-en, bread of heav-en, Feed me till I want no more.

D. C.

I am weak, but Thou art might-y, Hold me with Thy pow'rful hand:

2 Open now the crystal fountain,
  Whence the healing waters flow;
Let the fiery cloudy pillar
  Lead me all my journey through:
Strong Deliv'rer, strong Deliv'rer,
  Be Thou still my strength and shield.

3 When I tread the verge of Jordan,
  Bid my anxious fears subside;
Bear me through the swelling current,
  Land me safe on Canaan's side:
Songs of praises, songs of praises,
  I will ever give to Thee.

No. 30. I Want to be a Worker.

I. B.

I. HALTZELL. By per.

1. I want to be a work-er for the Lord; I want to love and trust His ho - ly word; I want to sing and pray, and be toil - ing ev - 'ry day In the vine - yard of the Lord.
2. I want to be a work-er ev - 'ry day; I want to lead the err - ing in the way That leads to heav'n a - bove, where all is peace and love, In the king - dom of the Lord.
3. I want to be a work-er strong and brave; I want to trust in Je - sus' pow'r to save; All who will tru - ly come, shall find a hap - py home In the king - dom of the Lord.
4. I want to be a work-er: help me Lord, To lead the lost and err - ing to Thy word That points to joys on high, where pleas-ures nev - er die In the king - dom of the Lord.

CHORUS.

I will work, I will pray, In the vine-yard, in the
I will work and pray, I will work and pray,

vine-yard of the Lord, (of the Lord;) I will work, I will pray,

I Want to be a Worker. Concluded.

I will la-bor ev-'ry day In the vine-yard of the Lord.

No. 31. We'll Never Say Good By.

"We shall never say 'good by' in heaven."—The words of a dying Christian Woman.

Mrs. E. W. CHAPMAN.   J. H. TENNEY.

1. Our friends on earth we meet with pleasure, While swift the moments fly,
2. How joy-ful is the tho't that lin-gers, When lov'd ones cross death's sea,
3. No part-ing words shall e'er be spok-en In that bright land of flow'rs,

Yet ev-er comes the tho't of sad-ness That we must say good by.
That when our la-bors here are end-ed, With them we'll ev-er be.
But songs of joy, and peace, and glad-ness, Shall ev-er-more be ours.

CHORUS.

We'll nev-er say good by in heav'n, We'll nev-er say good by, (good by,)

Repeat Chorus pp.

For in that land of joy and song We'll nev-er say good by.

No. 32.   I Can Not Tell Why.

Rev. John McPhail.   M. L. McPhail.

1. I can not tell why the dear Sav-ior should love me, Or why He should
2. But when I con-sid-er the grand con-de-scen-sion, The great blood-y
3. I look up-on Je-sus sur-round-ed by sin-ners, I look up-on
4. I won-der if an-gels can tell the deep meaning Of such con-de-

come from His throne in the sky, I can not ex-plain the great
sweat in the gar-den at night, The sor-row-ful heart, and the
Him as He hangs on the tree, I hear the pe-ti-tion, "Oh
scen-sion of this love so free, Or does it not reach far be-

rea-son He suf-fered For such a poor sin-ner, un-worth-y as I.
cup of de-ris-ion, I stand in a-maze-ment and wit-ness the sight.
Fa-ther, for-give them, For-give them for all that they do un-to me."
yond all con-cep-tion, Re-main-ing a bound-less and fath-om-less sea.

CHORUS.

He loves me, I know it, tho' help-less and poor, For noth-ing is

plain-er to me, I am sure; But why He should love me to

I Can Not Tell Why. Concluded.

suf-fer and die, I an-swer, I know not, I can not tell why.

No. 33. Fill Me Now.

E. H. STOKES. D. D.

JNO. R. SWENEY. By per.

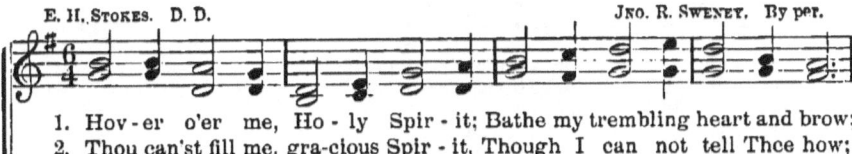

1. Hov-er o'er me, Ho - ly Spir - it; Bathe my trembling heart and brow;
2. Thou can'st fill me, gra-cious Spir - it, Though I can not tell Thee how;
3. I am weak-ness, full of weak-ness; At Thy sa - cred feet I bow;
4. Cleanse and comfort, bless and save me; Bathe, oh, bathe my heart and brow;

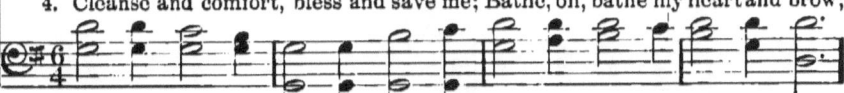

FINE.

Fill me with Thy hal-lowed pres-ence, Come, oh, come and fill me now.
But I need Thee, great-ly need Thee; Come, oh, come and fill me now.
Blest, di - vine, e - ter - nal Spir - it, Fill with pow'r, and fill me now.
Thou art com - fort - ing and sav - ing, Thou art sweet-ly fill - ing now.

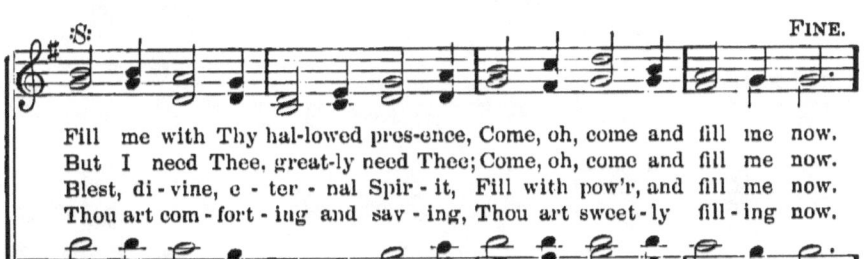

D.S. Fill me with Thy hallow'd presence, Come, oh, come and fill me now.

CHORUS.

D.S.

Fill me now, fill me now, Je - sus, come and fill me now.

No. 34. I'll Tell It.

Arr. by E. F. M.

E. F. MILLER.

1. Noth-ing to say for Je - sus, When He has done all for me?
2. Noth-ing to say for Je - sus, When sin-ners in-quire to know?
3. Noth-ing to say for Je - sus, A-shamed of my Sav-ior now?

Noth-ing to say for Je - sus, Who suf-fered on Cal - va - ry,
Noth-ing to say for Je - sus, And tell them what they must do,
Noth-ing to say for Je - sus, Not e - ven His name a - vow?

Re-deem-ing my soul from sor - row, And fit - ting it for the skies?
To flee from the wrath that's coming—Es - cap-ing the judg-ment day,—
And does He not plain - ly tell me, "If thou wilt say naught for me,

Oh! how can I then be si - lent, In view of the sac - ri - fice?
To taste of His great sal - va - tion? Oh! shall I have this to say?
In glo - ry, be-fore my Fa-ther, I will not say aught for thee?"

CHORUS.

I'll tell.............. it, I'll tell.............. it, How

Tell it to all, Tell it to all, How

From "The Shout of Victory," by per.

I'll Tell It. Concluded.

pre-cious a ran-som, He gave;.......... I'll tell.......... of His

pre-cious a ran-som, the ran-som He gave; Tell of His love,

love,............

Tell of His love, And His won-der-ful pow-er to save.

No. 35. Arise, My Soul.

C. WESLEY.

J EDSON. 1782.

1. A-rise, my soul, a-rise: Shake off thy guilty fears, The bleeding sac-ri-
2. He ev-er lives a-bove, For me to in-ter-cede, His all re-deem-ing
3. To God now rec-on-ciled; His pardoning voice I hear; He owns me for His

fice In my be-half ap-pears: Be-fore the throne my Sure-ty stands, Be-
love, His pre-cious blood to plead: His blood a-toned for all our race, His
child, I can no long-er fear; With con-fi-dence I now draw nigh, With

fore the throne my Sure-ty stands, My name is writ-ten on His hands.
blood a-toned for all our race, And sprinkles now the throne of grace.
con-fi-dence I now draw nigh, And Fa-ther, Ab-ba, Fa-ther, cry.

No. 36. At the Cross I'll Abide.

I. B.

I. BALTZELL.

1. O Je - sus, Sav - ior, I long to rest Near the
2. My dy - ing Je - sus, my Sav - ior God, Who hast
3. O Je - sus, Sav - ior, now make me Thine, Nev - er
4. The cleansing pow'r of Thy blood ap - ply, All my

cross where Thou hast died; For there is hope for the ach - ing breast,
borne my guilt and sin, Now wash me, cleanse me with Thine own blood,
let me stray from Thee; Oh, wash and cleanse me, for Thou art mine,
guilt and sin re - move, Oh, help me while at Thy cross I lie,

CHORUS.

At the cross I will a - bide. At the cross, I'll a -
Ev - er keep me pure and clean.
And Thy love is full and free.
Fill my soul with per - fect love. At the cross,

bide, At the cross, I'll a - bide, At the cross I'll a - bide,
I'll a - bide, At the cross, I'll a - bide,

There His blood is ap - plied; At the cross I am sanc - ti - fied.

By permission.

No. 37. The Waters of Jordan may Roll.

B. B.

BALLINGTON BOOTH.

1. The waves of death's riv-er are dark and cold, But Je-sus Him-
2. On this side the riv-er is war and strife 'Gainst sin by
3. On this side the riv-er a heav'n-ly peace Is of-fered to
4. As we ford the riv-er in sight of the land, Our loved ones will

self has pass'd thro'; The Sav-ior in mer-cy thy hand will hold:
God's faith-ful few, Yet trem-bling sin-ners are en-t'ring life,
you and to me; From doubting and sin there is sweet re-lease,
wel-come us o'er; We'll clasp their hands on the shin-ing strand,

CHORUS.

His prom-ise is faith-ful and true.
The pow'r that will car-ry them thro'. Oh, the wa-ters of
Till cross-ing with Je-sus to be.
And sing on the gold-en shore.

Jor-dan may roll, But Je-sus will car-ry me through;

His peace is now fill-ing my soul, Oh, that it were giv-en to you!

By permission.

No. 38.   Take me As I Am.

P. BILHORN.

1. Je-sus, my Lord, to Thee I cry, Un-less Thou help me, I must die,
2. Help-less I am, and full of guilt, But yet for me Thy blood was spilt,
3. If Thou hast work for me to do, In-spire my will, my heart re-new,
4. And when at last the work is done, The bat-tle o'er, the vic-t'ry won,

Oh, bring Thy free sal-va-tion nigh, And take me as I am!
And Thou canst make me what Thou wilt, But take me as I am!
And work both in and by me too, But take me as I am!
Still, still my cry shall be a-lone, Oh, take me as I am!

CHORUS.

Take me as I am! Pre-cious, bleed-ing Lamb,

Lord, I give my-self to Thee, O take me as I am!

No. 39. Gather at the River.

ROBERT LOWRY. By per.

1. Shall we gath-er at the riv-er, Where bright an-gel feet have trod,
2. On the mar-gin of the riv-er, Dash-ing up its sil-ver spray,
3. Ere we reach the shining riv-er, Lay we ev-ery bur-den down;
4. Soon we'll reach the sil-ver riv-er, Soon our pil-grim-age will cease;

With its crys-tal tide for ev-er Flow-ing by the throne of God?
We will walk and wor-ship ev-er, All the hap-py, gold-en day.
Grace our spir-its will de-liv-er, And pro-vide a robe and crown.
Soon our hap-py hearts will quiv-er With the mel-o-dy of peace.

CHORUS.

Yes, we'll gather at the riv-er, The beau-ti-ful, the beau-ti-ful riv-er—

Gath-er with the saints at the riv-er That flows by the throne of God.

No. 40. Sweetly Resting.

Mary D. James.

W. Warren Bentley. By per.

1. In the rift - ed Rock I'm rest-ing, Safe-ly shel-tered I a-bide;
2. Long pur-sued by sin and sa-tan, Weary, sad, I long'd for rest;
3. Peace, which pass-eth un-der-standing, Joy, the world can nev-er give,
4. In the rift - ed Rock I'll hide me, Till the storms of life are past,

There no foes nor storms mo-lest me, While with-in the cleft I hide.
Then I found this heav'n-ly shel-ter, O-pen'd in my Sav-ior's breast.
Now in Je - sus I am find-ing; In His smiles of love I live.
All se-cure in this blest ref-uge, Heeding not the fierc-est blast.

REFRAIN.

Now I'm rest - ing, sweet-ly rest - ing, In the cleft once made for me;

Je-sus, bless-ed Rock of A - ges, I will hide my-self in Thee.

No. 41. Christ is Mine.

Miss Ada Blenkhorn.

P. Bilhorn.

1. Sing I will and sing I must, Christ, the Lord is mine;
2. I will tell each sad dened heart, Christ, the Lord is mine;
3. Songs of joy my heart doth sing, Christ, the Lord is mine;
4. I will sing for ev - er - more, Christ, the Lord is mine;

In His mer - cy I will trust, Trust His pow'r di - vine.
If from sin you now de - part Christ will then be thine.
To His cross my all I bring, All to Christ re - sign.
Praise His name, His cross a - dore; 'Tis a joy sub - lime.

CHORUS.

Christ is mine, yes, Christ is mine, Christ, the Lord is mine.

Christ is mine, yes, Christ is mine, Je - sus Christ is mine.

No. 42. The Bird with a Broken Wing.

ANON.

Arr by F. M. LAMB. By per.

1. I walked thro' the wood-land mead-ows, Where sweet the thrush-es sing:
2. I found a young life bro-ken By sin's se-ductive art;
3. But the bird with a bro-ken pin-ion Kept an-oth-er from the snare;

And found on a bed of moss-es, A bird with a bro-ken wing.
And touched with a Christ-like pit-y I took him to my heart.
And the life that sin hath stricken Raised an-oth-er from de-spair.

I heal-ed its wound, and each morn-ing It sang its old sweet strain;
He lived with a no-ble pur-pose, And strug-gled not in vain:
Each loss has its com-pen-sa-tion, There is healing for ev-'ry pain:

But the bird with a bro-ken pin-ion, Nev-er soared as high a-gain.
But the life that sin hath strick-en, Nev-er soared as high a-gain.
But the bird with a bro-ken pin-ion, Nev-er soars as high a-gain.

No. 43. Able to Save and Keep.

C. E. G.

P. Bilhorn.

1. He's a - ble to keep you from fall - ing, He's a - ble all
2. He's a - ble to heal our dis - eas - es, Our bod - ies if
3. He's a - ble to car - ry our bur - dens, To rid us of
4. God's tho'ts to His chil - dren are pre - cious, All this and much

things to sub - due, To bind up the brok - en in
maimed, He'll make whole; He's a - ble to keep us from
all anx - ious care; He's a - ble to rest us when
more will He give; Thro' faith in the dear name of

Chorus.

spir - it, And save to the ut - ter-most too.
sin - ning, And per - fect His life in the soul. } A - ble,
wea - ry, He's will - ing our cross - es to share.
Je - sus, We ask and thro' Him we re - ceive.

A - ble to save,

will - ing, a - ble and will - ing to save, A - ble,

a - ble to keep, A - ble to save,

will - ing, Je - sus is a - ble to save.

a - ble to keep,

No. 44. My Mother's Hands.

Mrs. M. E. W.

Mrs. M. E. Willson.
Sister of the late P. P. Bliss.

Slow and with great expression.

1. Oh, those beau-ti-ful, beau-ti-ful hands! Tho' they neither were white nor small,
2. Oh, those beau-ti-ful, beau-ti-ful hands! How they cared for my in - fant days!
3. Oh, those beau-ti-ful, beau-ti-ful hands! As they pressed my ach - ing brow,
4. Oh, those beau-ti-ful, beau-ti-ful hands! Thin and wrinkled with age they grew;
5. Oh, those beau-ti-ful, beau-ti-ful hands! I stood by her cof-fin one day,
6. Oh, those beau-ti-ful, beau-ti-ful hands! I shall clasp them a - gain once more,

Yet my moth-er's hands were the fair - est And lov-li-est hands of all.
They guid-ed my feet in - to pleasant paths, And smoothed all the rug - ged ways.
They cooled the fe - ver and eased the pain, Me-thinks I can feel them now.
But still they toiled on for the child so dear, And her love seem'd more tender and true.
And I kissed those hands so cold and white, As qui-et and peace-ful she lay.
As my feet touch the bank of the heav'n-ly land; We shall meet on that shin - ing shore.

CHORUS.

My mother's dear hands, her beautiful hands, Which guided me safe o'er life's sands,

By permission.

My Mother's Hands. Concluded.

I bless God's name for the mem-'ry Of moth-er's own beau-ti-ful hands.

No. 45. Revive Us Again.

Dr. W. P. Mackay.

English Melody.

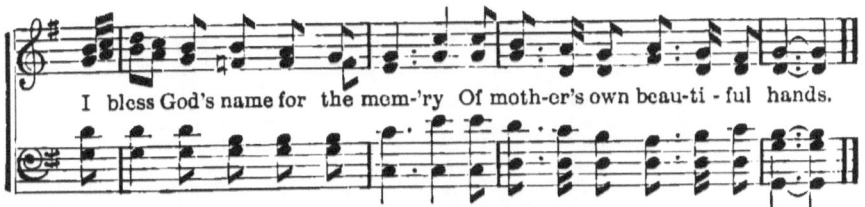

1. We praise Thee, O God! for the Son of Thy love, For
2. We praise Thee, O God! for Thy Spir-it of light, Who has
3. All glo-ry and praise to the Lamb that was slain, Who has

CHORUS.

Je-sus who died, and is now gone a-bove. Hal-le-lu-jal
shown us our Sav-ior, and scat-tered our night. Hal-le-lu-jal
borne all our sins, and has cleansed ev-'ry stain. Hal-le-lu-jal

Thine the glo-ry, Hal-le-lu-jah! A-men. Re-vive us a-gain.

4. All glory and praise to the God of all grace,
   Who has bought us, and sought us, and guided our ways.

5. Revive us again; fill each heart with Thy love;
   May each soul be rekindled with fire from above.

No. 46. Say, Are You Ready?

A. S. KIEFFER.

T. C. O'KANE.

1. Should the Death an - gel knock at thy cham - ber, In the still
2. Ma - ny sad spir - its now are de - part - ing In - to the
3. Ma - ny re - deemed ones now are as - cend - ing In - to the

watch of to - night, Say, will your spir - it pass in - to tor-ment,
world of de - spair; Ev - 'ry brief mo-ment brings your doom near-er;
man-sions of light; Je - sus is plead-ing, pa-tient - ly plead-ing,

CHORUS.

Or to the land of de - light?
Sin - ner, O sin - ner, be - ware!
Oh, let Him save you to - night.

Say, are you read - y,

Oh, are you read - y? If the Death an - gel should call, should call;

Say, are you read-y? Oh, are you read-y? Mer-cy stands waiting for all.

By permission.

No. 47. A Voice From the Billow.

Neva Parkhill Prentice.

P. Bilhorn.

1. A voice from the bil-low is call-ing, A dear one is drift-ing a-way, But her voice o'er the bil-low is fall-ing, And it sounds, mid the foam and the spray.

2. A light on the o-cean is dy-ing, A star pass-es in-to the night: But her bark, mid the tem-pest is fly-ing, Far a-way to the shores of de-light.

3. A hope that was born mid earth's sor-row, Hath held her with hands all di-vine; Thro' the pain of death's dawn-ing to-mor-row, Still the light of e-ter-ni-ty shines.

4. There the hun-ger, the heart-wea-ry striv-ing, The deep rest-less long-ings are gone; And the soul finds the glo-ry of liv-ing, In a land where the Lord is the sun.

CHORUS.

She is near-ing the beau-ti-ful cit-y, Where nev-er-more wea-ry she'll roam: Still her voice from the bil-low is call-ing, Come fol-low me, fol-low me home, (me home.)

4

No. 48.   Waiting for Me.

FRANK HENDRICKS.   JNO. R. SWENEY.

1. I came to the fountain that cleanseth from sin, The life-giv-ing
2. He saw me ap-proach-ing and ten-der-ly said: To pur-chase thy
3. I flew to His mer-cy, O joy-ful sur-prise, For lo, my Re-
4. And now in His pres-ence I walk with de-light, And feel His pro-

fount-ain, where millions have been; I came in my weak-ness, o'er-
ran-som my blood I have shed; And if thou art will-ing just
deem-er had o-pened my eyes; I flew to the ref-uge no
tec-tion by day and by night; I think of the fount-ain, so

burdened with care, To find my Re-deem er and Sav-ior was there.
now to be-lieve, The light of my Spir-it thy soul shall re-ceive.
oth-er could give, And faith-ful-ly prom-ised for Je-sus to live.
pre-cious and free, Where Je-sus my Sav-ior was wait-ing for me.

CHORUS.

Wait - - ing for me,............ wait - - ing for
Wait-ing for me, wait-ing for me, wait-ing for me,

ine,............ Je - - sus my Sav - - ior is
wait-ing for me, Je-sus my Sav-ior is wait-ing for me,

Waiting for Me. Concluded.

wait - - - ing for me,............. Still........... at the
Je - sus my Sav-ior is wait-ing for me; Still at the fount

fount......... oft............. would I be,............. Where
oft would I be, Still at the fount oft would I be, Where

Je - - - sus my Sav - ior is wait - ing for me.
Je-sus my Sav-ior is waiting for me, is waiting, is waiting for me.

No. 49.   Heavenly Bread.

CARLE.

P. BILHORN.

Je - sus, Sav-ior, Heav'n-ly Bread, While this earth-ly path we tread,

Feed, in-struct, sup-port, de-fend, Safe-ly lead us to the end.   A - men.

No. 50. In the Depths of the Sea.

PETER BILHORN. Micah 7: 19. J. H. TENNEY.

1. I will cast in the depths of the fath-om-less sea,
2. In the great un-known depths, where the storms nev-er sweep,
3. In the dark, si-lent depths, far a-way from the shore,
4. So re-joice all ye ran-somed, a-way from the light

All thy sins and trans-gres-sions what-ev-er they be:
All thy sins have been cast in the grave of the deep,
Where they nev-er can rise up to trou-ble thee more,
All thy sins have been hid-den, thy fu-ture is bright:

Though they mount up to heav-en or reach down to hell,
Where no mor-tal can en-ter thy faults to de-ride,
Where no far-reach-ing tide, with its ter-ri-ble roar,
Far a-bove them the waves of His mer-cy doth flow,

They shall sink in the depths, and a-bove them shall swell
Far a-bove them for-ev-er flows love's might-y tide;
Ev-er stir the dark waves of for-get-ful-ness o'er,
For He lov-eth to par-don, and grace to be-stow;

In the Depths of the Sea. Concluded.

All my waves of for - give - ness, so might - y and free,
Of that sep - ul - chre vast I a - lone hold the key,
I have bur - ied them there thro' all a - ges to be:
Yea, thy sins, tho' as scar - let or crim - son they be,

Rit. - - - - - - -

"I will cast all thy sins in the depths of the sea."
And I bur - ied them there in the depths of the sea.
I have cast all thy sins in the depths of the sea.
He for - ev - er has cast in the depths of the sea.

No. 51. Lift Me Higher.

G. W. L.   G. W. Lyon.

1. Lift me high - er, Sav - ior, Near - er to Thy throne,
2. I am poor and need - y, Weak and full of sin;
3. Guide my fee - ble foot - steps Thro' this world of strife,
4. Let Thy grace il - lu - mine My be - night - ed soul,

Make me pur - er, bet - ter, Make me Thine a - lone.
Make me meek and hum - ble, Je - sus dwell with - in.
Help me on - ward, Sav - ior, To a bet - ter life.
Come, Thy - self pos - sess it, Take and make me whole.

No One but Jesus.

P. B.

P. BILHORN.

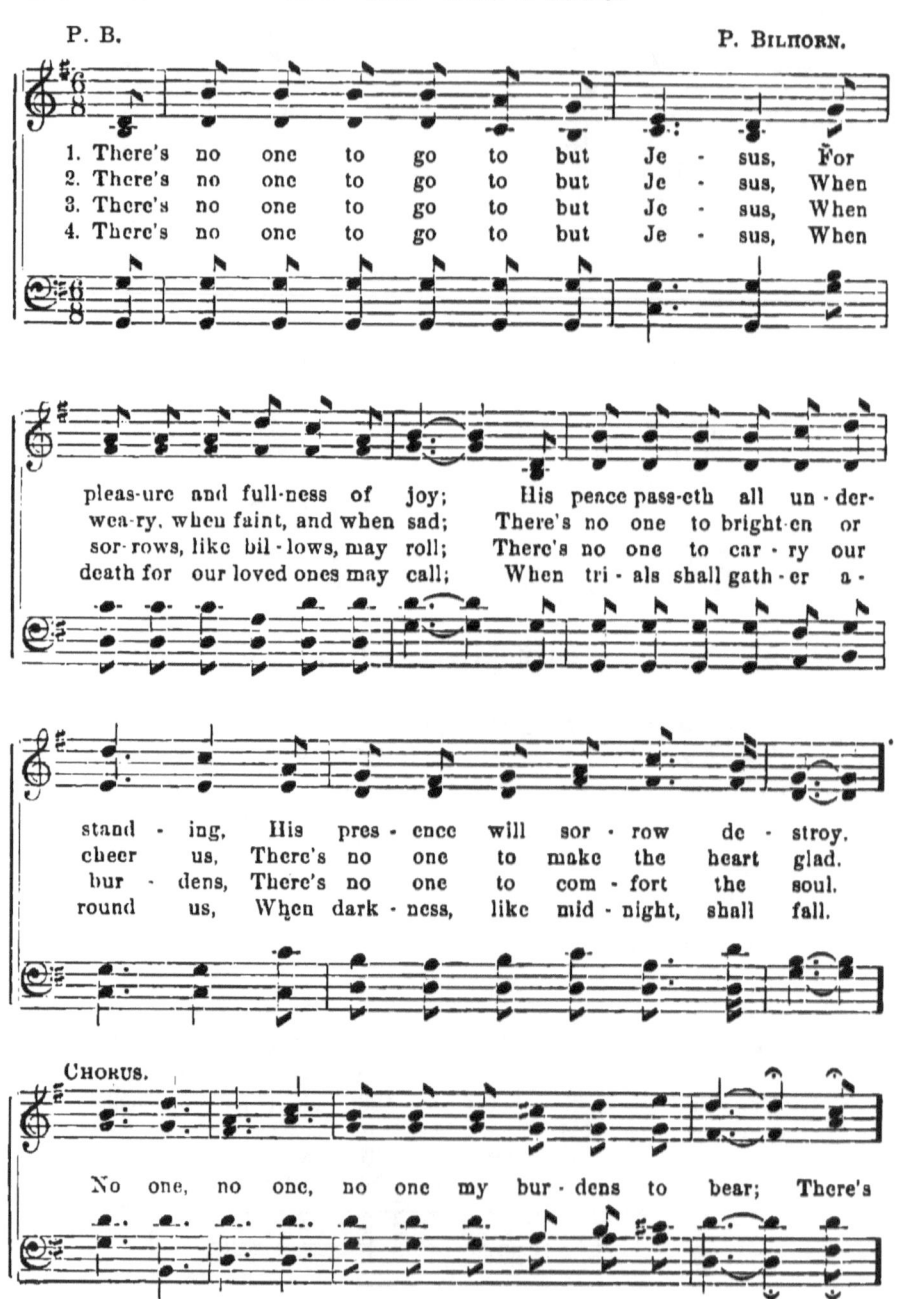

1. There's no one to go to but Je - sus, For
2. There's no one to go to but Je - sus, When
3. There's no one to go to but Je - sus, When
4. There's no one to go to but Je - sus, When

pleas-ure and full-ness of joy; His peace pass-eth all un-der-
wea-ry, when faint, and when sad; There's no one to bright-en or
sor-rows, like bil-lows, may roll; There's no one to car-ry our
death for our loved ones may call; When tri - als shall gath-er a-

stand - ing, His pres - ence will sor - row de - stroy.
cheer us, There's no one to make the heart glad.
bur - dens, There's no one to com - fort the soul.
round us, When dark - ness, like mid - night, shall fall.

CHORUS.

No one, no one, no one my bur - dens to bear; There's

No One but Jesus. Concluded.

no one to go to but Je·sus, There's no one my sor·rows to share.

No. 53. I Know.

Miss J. H. JOHNSTON.   P. BILHORN.

1. I know   the   Re·deem·er   is   might·y,   His
2. For par·don, for peace, and for cleans·ing,   I
3. His grace will a·vail for the low·est,   And

grace and His mer·cy are free; When I was a stran·ger He
bring but His Name as my plea; His blood hath a·toned for the
all who will trust Him will see How great is the love of the

sought me, He came, in His mer··cy to me.
sin·ner,   That foun·tain was o·pened for me.
Sav·ior,   Who ran·somed a sin·ner like me.

4 The wonderful gift of salvation,
   I know He will give unto thee;
He longs in His love to bestow it,
   I know—for He gave it to me.

5 His servants at last shall behold Him;
   O gracious and royal decree!
To you is the glad invitation,
   Come, trust Him, and meet Him with me

No. 54.   Come and Be Saved.

C. H. G.

CHAS. H. GABRIEL. By per.

1 There's an in-vi-ta-tion from a-bove, Come and be saved,
2. Are you wea-ry, are you sore op-prest? Come and be saved,
3. Je-sus of-fers you sal-va-tion free, Come and be saved.

Come and be saved; Je-sus bids you to the feast of love, Come and be
Come and be saved; Je-sus of-fers you a per-fect rest, Come and be
Come and be saved; To the shel-ter of His mer-cy flee, Come and be

saved. Tho' your sins be scar-let, sin-ner, come, Je-sus bids the wand'ring
saved. Out of dark-ness in-to glo-rious light, Out of sad-ness in-to
saved. In His bless-ed word He bids you come, In His mer-cy there is

soul come home; Why in sor-row will you long-er roam? Come and be saved.
strange de-light, Out of bondage, out of gloom and night, Come and be saved.
ev-er room For the prod-i-gal who seeks a home, Come and be saved.

We Walk by Faith.

J. E. WOLFE.   P. BILHORN.

1. By child-like faith in Christ, the Lord, We have from sin salvation;
2. How simple is the way of life, 'Tis only to believe Him;
3. Thro' Jesus' death the debt was paid, Not feeling, nor emotion,
4. We walk by faith and not by sight, How grand is this revealing!

By fully trusting in His word, We pass from condemnation.
'Twill end your sorrow and your strife If you will but receive Him.
On Him our sin and guilt was laid; O, give Him your devotion.
'Tis God's own way, and must be right, 'Tis wrong to trust in feeling.

CHORUS.

We walk by faith, and not by sight;
We walk by faith and not by sight; 'Tis God's own way and must be right;

We walk by faith,
We walk by faith and not by sight; We follow Christ, the Light.

No. 56. Yes, for Me.

Words arranged.

ENGLISH.

1. Yes, for me, for me He car-eth With a broth-er's ten-der care,
2. Yes, for me, for me He watcheth, Ceaseless watcheth night and day,
3. Yes, for me, for me He pleadeth, At the mer-cy seat a-bove,

Yes, for me, for me He bear-eth Ev-ery bur-den, ev-ery care;
Yes, e'en me, e'en me He snatch-eth From the per-ils by the way;
Yes, for me He in-ter-ced-eth At the Fa-ther's throne of love;

REFRAIN.

Ev-ery bur-den, ev-ery bur-den, Ev-ery bur-den, ev-ery care,
From the per-ils, from the per-ils, From the per-ils by the way,
With the Fa-ther, with the Fa-ther In the heav'n-ly courts a-bove,

Yes, for me, for me He bear-eth Ev-ery bur-den, ev-ery care.
Yes, e'en me, e'en me He snatcheth From the per-ils by the way.
Yes, for me He in-ter-ced-eth At the Fa-ther's throne of love.

No. 57. For Christ and the Church.

E. E. HEWITT.   WM. J. KIRKPATRICK.

1. For Christ and the church, let our voi - ces ring, Let us hon - or the
2. For Christ and the church, be our earn - est pray'r, Let us fol - low His
3. For Christ and the church, willing off'rings make, Time and tal - ents and
4. For Christ and the church, let us cast a - side, By His con-quer-ing

name of our own bless - ed King, Let us work with a will in the
ban - ner, the cross dai - ly bear, Let us yield, whol-ly yield, to His
gold, for the dear Mas-ter's sake; We'll re-mem - ber the best we can
grace, chains of self, fear, and pride; May our lives be en-riched by an

strength of youth, And loy - al - ly stand for the king - dom of truth.
Spir-it's pow'r, And faith - ful - ly serve Him in life's brightest hour.
bring to Him, The heart's wealth of love, that will nev - er grow dim.
aim so grand, Then hap - py the call to the Sav - ior's right hand.

CHORUS.

For Christ our dear Re-deemer, For Christ who died to save;
For Christ   For Christ

For the Church His blood hath purchased, Lord, make us pure and brave.
For the Church

No. 58. Prepare to Meet Thy God.

P. B.

P. BILHORN.

1. Pre-pare to meet thy God, Ere judg-ment He doth send; E-
2. Pre-pare to meet thy God, He soon may sum-mon thee To
3. Pre-pare to meet thy God, Ere death may call for thee; Pre-
4. Pre-pare to meet thy God, While mer - cy yet is near: For

ter - ni-ty is draw-ing near, The day of grace will end.
come be-fore His judg-ment seat; What will thy an-swer be?
pare, my broth-er, ere you're lost. Thro' all e - ter-ni-ty.
par-don, look un-to the blood, This warn-ing voice now hear.

CHORUS. m   f

Pre - pare to meet thy God, Pre - pare to meet thy God, The

ff   p Rit. - - - - - -

day of grace will soon be gone, Pre-pare to meet thy God.

No. 59. The Three-fold Look.

H. G. SMEAD. P. BILHORN.

1. I back-ward look to Cal - va - ry, 'Twas there the debt was paid;
2. I look a - round, my pres - ent need The ris - en Lord doth know:
3. I for - ward look, my heart is thrilled With earn-est of His power;
4. Dark doubts and fears ne'er cloud the sun Of him with mind thus stayed:

By God's own Son, who died for me, 'Twas there my peace was made.
Sus - tain - ing grace for me He'll plead, To do His will be - low.
His com - ing will be joy ful - filled; Oh, haste the bless - ed hour!
The se - cret springs of heav'n be - gun, This three-fold look is made.

CHORUS. *Cres.* - - - - - -

Then look! look! look! Then look to Him and live, . . . And

you shall see He died for thee, E - ter - nal life to give.

No. 60.   Papa, Come this Way.

(A fisherman got lost in the fog; his little child called from the shore: "Come this way:" and, guided by the voice, he reached home in safety. So, unsaved and lost fathers, listen to little voices from the heavenly shore, calling: "Papa, come this way.")

M. E. W.

Mrs. M. E. Willson.
Arr. by Alfred Beirly.

DUET.

1. A lit-tle childish voice is still'd, Two little lily-white hands are crossed:
2. I'm sure my dar-ling is at rest, With-in the ten-der Shep-herd's fold;
3. Wher-e'er I go, that voice I hear, As tho' my dar-ling could not rest,

ORGAN.

Two lit-tle eyes for-ev-er closed, The sound of pat-t'ring feet is lost,
He took her from this sinful world, He shields her from its blast and cold.
Un-til I give my heart to Him, Who died to save and make me blest.

Rit.

A lit-tle form from out our home, Was borne by lov-ing hands a-way;
But how I miss the lov-ing kiss, And oh! my long-ing heart is sore;
And so it ech-oes in my heart, And thro' the chambers of my soul,

But still I seem to hear a voice With-in my heart it says each day,
Then comes that pleading little voice, It gen-tly whis-pers o'er and o'er,
I'll not resist that pleading voice, *I'll go to Je-sus and be whole.*

CHORUS.

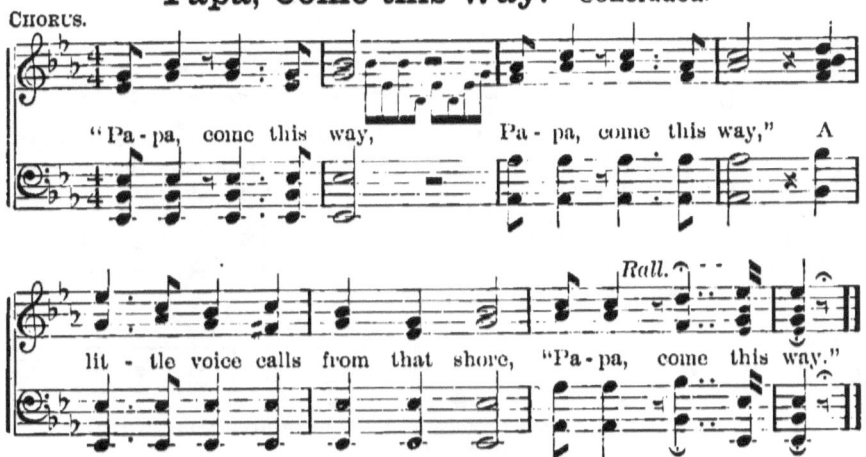

"Pa-pa, come this way, Pa-pa, come this way," A

lit-tle voice calls from that shore, "Pa-pa, come this way."

No. 61. Come, Thou Fount.

Rev. R. Robinson, 1758. NETTLETON. Old Melody. 1812.

FINE.

1. { Come, Thou Fount of ev-'ry bless-ing, Tune my heart to sing Thy grace; }
   { Streams of mer-cy, nev-er ceas-ing, Call for songs of loud-est praise; }
D. C. Praise the mount, I'm fixed up-on it! Mount of Thy re-deem-ing love.

D. C.

Teach me some me-lo-dious son-net, Sung by flam-ing tongues a-bove;

2 Here I'll raise my Ebenezer,
   Hither by Thy help I'm come;
And I hope by Thy good pleasure,
   Safely to arrive at home.
Jesus sought me when a stranger,
   Wandering from the fold of God;
He to rescue me from danger
   Interposed His precious blood.

3 Oh, to grace how great a debtor,
   Daily I'm constrained to be!
Let Thy goodness as a fetter,
   Bind my wandering heart to Thee;
Prone to wander, Lord, I feel it—
   Prone to leave the God I love—
Here's my heart, oh, take and seal it,
   Seal it for Thy courts above.

No. 62. Bring Them In.

ALEXCENAH THOMAS. W. A. OGDEN.

1. Hark! 'tis the Shepherd's voice I hear, Out in the des-ert
2. Who'll go and help this Shepherd kind, Help Him the lit - tle
3. Out in the des - ert, hear their cry, Out on the mountain

dark and drear, Call - ing the lambs who've gone a - stray,
lambs to find? Who'll bring the lost ones to the fold?
wild and high, Hark! 'tis the Mas - ter speaks to thee:

CHORUS.

Far from the Shep-herd's fold a - way.
Where they'll be shel - tered from the cold.   Bring them in,
"Go, find my lambs, wher - e'er they be."

Bring them in,   Bring them in from the fields of sin;

Bring them in,   Bring them in.   Bring the lit - tle ones to Je - sus.

No. 63. Cast Thy Burden on the Lord.

W J. K. I Peter, 5: 7. WM. J. KIRKPATRICK.

1 Wea-ry pil-grim on life's path-way, Strug-gling on be-neath thy load;
2. Are thy tir-ed feet un-stead-y? Does thy lamp no light af-ford?
3 Are the ties of friend-ship sev-ered? Hush'd the voic-es fond-ly heard?
4 Does thy heart with faintness fal-ter? Does thy mind for-get His word?
5. He will hold thee up from fall-ing, He will guide thy steps a-right;

Hear these words of con-so-la-tion, "Cast thy bur-den on the Lord."
Is thy cross too great and heav-y? Cast thy bur-den on the Lord.
Breaks thy heart with weight of an-guish, Cast thy bur-den on the Lord.
Does thy strength suc-cumb to weak-ness? Cast thy bur-den on the Lord.
He will strength-en each en-deav-or; He will keep thee by His might.

CHORUS.

Cast thy bur-den on the Lord, Cast thy bur-den on the Lord, And He will

strengthen thee, sus-tain and com-fort thee; Cast thy bur-den on the Lord.

5

No. 64. Jesus Will Save You Now.

JULIA H. JOHNSTON.　　　　　　　　　　　　　　　　P. BILHORN.

1. Je - sus, the Lord who was cru - ci - fied, Je - sus will save you now. You are the sin - ner for whom He died, Je - sus will save you now, Lov - ing you ten - der - ly long a - go, Leav - ing His home for the earth be - low, None oth - er

2. Friends and com - pan - ions may give you love, Je - sus a - lone can save; This will not bear you in peace a - bove, Je - sus a - lone can save. Why should you wait for a loud - er call? Why should you lin - ger till clouds ap - pall? Hast - en to

3. This is the time, the ac - cept - ed time, Je - sus is call - ing now, Come un - to Him, ere the last hour chime, Je - sus is call - ing now. Come for the mo - ments are fly - ing fast. Soon will the sea - son be o - ver - past, Come, for the

4. Peace in be - liev - ing you now may claim, Trust in your Sav - ior now; Per - fect re - demp - tion is through His name, Trust in the Sav - ior now. Ho - ly and harm - less and un - de - filed, Wait - ing for you to be rec - on - ciled, Come to Him

Jesus Will Save You Now. Concluded.

Sav - ior your heart may know, Je - sus will save you now.
Him, ere the dark - ness fall, Je - sus a - lone can save.
door shall be closed at last, Je - sus is call - ing now.
now as a lit - tle child, Trust in your Sav - ior now.

No. 65. Duke Street.

J. HATTON.

1. O God, be - neath Thy guid - ing hand, Our ex - iled
2. What change! thro' path - less wilds no more The fierce and
3. Laws, free - dom, truth, and faith in God Came with those
4. And here Thy name, O God of love, Their chil - dren's

fa - thers crossed the sea, And when they trod the
na - ked sav - age roams: Sweet praise, a - long the
ex - iles o'er the waves, And where their pil - grim
chil - dren shall a - dore, Till these e - ter - nal

win - try strand, With pray'r and psalm they wor-shiped Thee.
cul - tured shore, Breaks from ten thou - sand hap - py homes.
feet have trod, The God they trust - ed guards their graves.
hills re - move, And spring a - dorns the earth no more.

No. 66. The Penitent's Plea.

H. H. B.

Commandant H. H. Booth.

Andante con espress.

1. Sav - ior, hear me, while be - fore Thy feet I the
   Canst Thou still in mer - cy think of me, Stoop to
2. All the mem - o - ries of deeds gone by Rise with-
   Sav - ior, take my hand, I can - not tell How to
3. Yet why should I fear, hast Thou not died That no
   By the love and pit - y Thou hast shown, By the

rec - ord of my sins re - peat, Stained with guilt, my-self ab-
set my shackled spir - it free, [Omit.]
in me and Thy pow'r de - fy; With a death-ly chill en-
stem the tides that round me swell, [Omit.]
seek-ing soul should be de - nied? To that heart its sins con-
blood that did for me a - tone, [Omit.]

1st time.

hor - ring, Filled with grief, my soul out-pour - ing;
snar - ing, They would leave my soul de-spair - ing.
fess - ing, Canst Thou fail to give a bless - ing?

2d time. Cres.

Raise my sink-ing heart, and bid me be Thy child
How to ease my con-science or to quell My flam -
Bold - ly will I kneel be - fore Thy throne, A plead -

Dim. - - - -

The Penitent's Plea. Concluded.

CHORUS. mp

once more?
ing heart.
ing soul.

Grace there is my ev'-ry debt to pay,

Cres.

Blood to wash my ev-'ry sin a-way, Pow'r to

Dim.

keep me sinless day by day, For me, for me!

4 All the rivers of Thy grace I claim,
Over ev'ry promise write my name;
As I am I come believing,
As Thou art Thou dost, receiving,

Bid me rise a free and pardon'd slave;
Master o'er my sin, the world, the grave,
Charging me to preach Thy power to
To sin-bound souls. [save

No. 67. My Soul, be on Thy Guard.

GEORGE HEATH.   Dr. LOWELL MASON.

1. My soul, be on thy guard; Ten thou-sand foes a - rise;
2. Oh, watch, and fight, and pray; The bat - tle ne'er give o'er;
3. Ne'er think the vic - t'ry won, Nor lay thine ar - mor down:

The hosts of sin are press-ing hard To draw thee from the skies.
Re - new it bold-ly ev - 'ry day, And help di - vine im - plore.
The work of faith will not be done, Till thou ob - tain the crown.

No. 68.   I Found Sweet Peace.

P. B.

C. EICKENBERG.

1. I found sweet peace in Christ my Lord, Which noth-ing can de-stroy;
2. There's joy su-preme with-in my soul, For Je-sus now is there;
3. Oh, troub-led one with sins dismayed, There's cleansing in the blood;

And as I ful-ly trust His word, My heart is filled with joy.
He drives all sor-row's tears a-way, My bur-dens He doth bear.
Then come to Christ, your debt He paid, Be rec-on-ciled to God.

I'll lean up-on His might-y arm, And in His strength I'll go;
I'll trust His prom-is-es of grace, And in His love I'll rest,
There's grace suf-fi-cient for thy need, Oh, come just as thou art;

With Him I'll fear no ill nor harm, He longs His grace to show.
Thro' tri-als dark be-hold His face, With Him I shall be blest.
For you, my broth-er, we now plead, To Christ give now thy heart.

More Like Jesus.

J. M. S.   J. M. STILLMAN.

1. I want to be more like Je - sus, And fol - low Him day by day:
2. I want to be kind and gen - tle, To those who are in dis - tress:
3. I want to be meek and low - ly, Like Je - sus, our Friend and King;
4. I want to be pure and ho - ly, As pure as the crys-tal snow;

I want to be true and faith - ful, And ev - 'ry com-mand o bey.
To com-fort the bro - ken heart- ed, With sweet words of ten-der - ness.
I want to be strong and earn - est, And souls to the Sav - ior bring.
I want to love Je - sus dear - ly, For Je - sus loves me, I know.

REFRAIN.

More and more like Je - sus, I would ev - er be,......
ev - er be,

More and more like Je - sus, My Sav - ior who died for me.

From "Goodwill," by per.

No. 70. Room in Heaven for Thee.

Mrs. F. Fistler.

P. Bilhorn.

1. How sad it would be, if when thou dost call, All hope-less and
2. How sad it would be, were the har-vest past, The bright summer
3. Oh, come to the Lord while His mer-cy's near, Re-mem-ber His

un-for-giv'n, The an-gel that stands at the beau-ti-ful gate Should
days all gone, To know that the reap-ers had gather'd the sheaves, And
life He gave; The love that has sought thee is seek-ing thee still, And

CHORUS.

an-swer, no room in heav'n. Sad, oh, how sad, no room in heav'n for
left thee to die a-lone. Sad, oh, how sad, etc.
Je-sus now waits to save. Yes, yes, there's room, there's room in heav'n for

thee, No room, (no room,) no room, (no room,) no room in heav'n for
thee, Then come, (oh, come,) then come, (yes, come,) there's room in heav'n for

thee; No room, (no room,) no room, (no room,) no room in heav'n for thee.
thee; Then come, (oh, come,) then come, (oh, come,) there's room in heav'n for thee.

No. 71.   We'll Meet Again.

Rev. H. G. Jackson, D. D.   Mrs. W. S. Nickle.

1. We'll meet a-gain the "lov'd and lost," Where partings rend the heart no more;
2. How sweet the welcome to that land; The ra-diant smile on each dear face;
3. That hap-py meet-ing will a-tone For all our un-a-vail-ing tears;
4. The lov'd, not lost! what bliss to meet And join with them in heav'ns em-ploy;

When we death's mys-tic stream have crossed, And moored our barks to yon-der shore.
The thrill-ing press-ure of the hand, The sud-den joy, the long em-brace!
While treading life's rude path a-lone Thro' ma-ny, wea-ry, joy-less years.
The dear Lord's praise, commun-ion sweet, And songs of ev-er-last-ing joy!

CHORUS.

O yes, we'll meet them on that shore, We'll meet where parting is no more;

All sor-rows past, all grief and pain; On that blest shore we'll meet a-gain!

No. 72. Holy Spirit, Guide, Revealer.

JULIA H. JOHNSTON.   P. BILHORN.

1. Ho - ly Spir - it, Guide, Re-veal - er, Let Thy light up - on us shine,
2. Fit our hearts for Thine in-dwell-ing, Spir - it of all truth and grace,
3. Give re - pent-ance and re - new - ing, Melt and move each hardened heart,

Show to us the things of Je - sus, Man - i - fest Thy pow'r di - vine.
Make of us Thine earth - ly tem - ples, Meet for Thine a - bid - ing place.
Give re - vi - val and re-fresh-ing, All our help and hope Thou art.

Let Thy quick'ning grace be giv - en, Teach our doubt-ing hearts to pray,
Let us share the sweet com-mun- ion, And the fel - low-ship of love;
Com-fort - er whom Je - sus prom-ised, Un - to Thee our hearts we raise:

Keep our way-ward feet from stray-ing, Lead us in the nar-row way.
Sanc - ti - fy and keep and com -fort-"Ho - ly Spir - it, heav'n-ly Dove."
One with Christ and with the Fa - ther, To Thy name be end-less praise.

No. 73. Singing All the Way.

J. H. K. J. H. KURZENKNABE.

1. 'Mid in - no - cence and joy - ous glee, At dawn of life's fair day,
2. In ten - der youth ere sor - row came, Ere tempters could be-tray,
3. Now in the strength of manhood's pride, When battling hosts ar-ray,
4. Should age bring heav - y bur-dens down, To life's long, wea - ry day,

My lov - ing Sav - ior cared for me, For this I sing to-day.
I learned to love the Sav - ior's name, For this I sing to-day.
My ref - uge is the flow - ing tide, For this I sing to-day.
There's rest be - yond, a robe, a crown, For this I sing to-day.

CHORUS.

I'm sing - ing, sing - ing,
I'm sing-ing on to vic - to - ry, I'm sing - ing ev - 'ry day;

To Him all glo - ry be,
To Him shall all the glo - ry be, I'm sing - ing all the way.

No. 74.　　　Oh, to be Something.

Rev. Geo. W. Crofts.　　　　　　　　　　　　　　　　　Arthur J. Smith.

1. Oh, to be some-thing, dear Sav - ior, I pray, Some-thing of
2. Some-thing, where spir - its are bur-dened with sin, Some-thing, those
3. Some-thing to o - pen the eyes of the blind, Some-thing to
4. Some-thing to sol - ace e - ter - ni - ty's fears, Some-thing to

use to the world in my day; Some-thing, dear Sav - ior, what-
spir - its for heav - en to win; Some-thing, to woo them to
light - en the sin-dark-ened mind; Some-thing, to lead them to
cheer when e - ter - ni - ty nears; Some-thing, to ban - ish death's

ev - er it be, Some-thing, yes some-thing of hon - or to Thee.
Cal - va - ry's cross, Some-thing, to give them pure gold for their dross.
foun-tains of love, Some-thing, to point them to man-sions a - bove.
ven - om - ous sting, Some-thing, to help them life's tri-umphs to sing.

CHORUS.

Oh, to be some - thing, my Sav - ior, do Thou Make of me

Copyright, 1889, by Arthur J. Smith. By per.

Oh, to be Something. Concluded.

some-thing, yes some-thing just now; Some-thing, dear Sav - ior, what-

ev - er it be, Some-thing, yes, some-thing of hon - or to Thee.

No. 75.   I Love Thy Church.

T. DWIGHT.   F. L. ARMSTRONG.

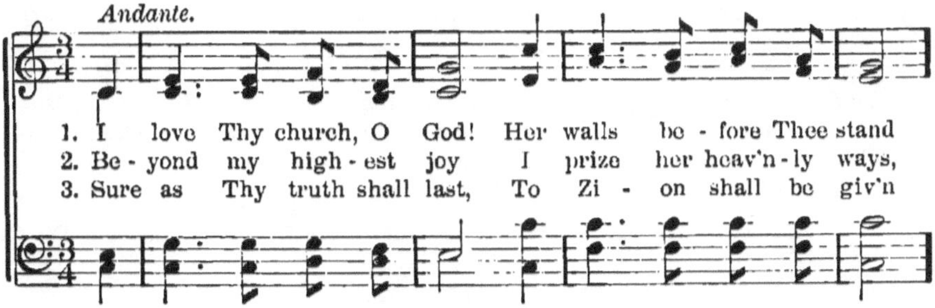

Andante.

1. I love Thy church, O God! Her walls be - fore Thee stand
2. Be - yond my high - est joy I prize her heav'n - ly ways,
3. Sure as Thy truth shall last, To Zi - on shall be giv'n

Ritard.

Dear as the ap - ple of Thine eye, And gra - ven on Thy hand.
Her sweet com-mun - ion, sol - emn vows, Her hymns of love and praise.
The bright-est glo - ries earth can yield, And bright - er bliss of heav'n.

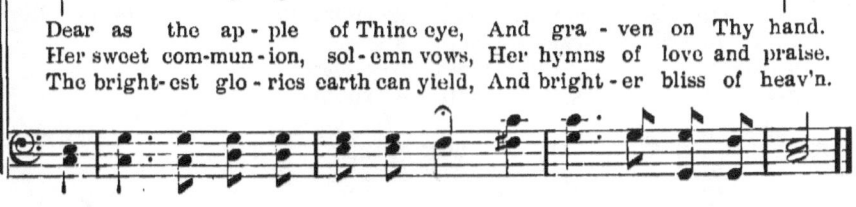

Christus Hath Arisen.

JULIA H. JOHNSTON.

P. BILHORN.

1. Sing, O my soul, re - peat the old - en sto - ry,
2. Spread, spread the news of Je - sus' res - ur - rec - tion,
3. O ris - en Lord, o'er life and death vic - to - rious,
4. He will re - turn! His prom - ise stands re - cord - ed;

Christ on the cross is slain for guilt-y men; Low in the grave, be-
Tell how the stone was quick-ly rolled a - way; Death could not hold its
Look from Thy throne on all who trust in Thee; By all Thy might, by
Each eye shall see and ev - 'ry heart shall burn; Still watch and wait, till

hold the Lord of glo - ry, Shout, shout the vic - to - ry! He
King in meek sub - jec - tion, Come, see the emp - ty tomb where
Thine as - cen - sion glo - rious, Thou art ex - alt - ed our Re-
faith and hope re - ward - ed, Sound out the tri - umph-note to

f CHORUS. *m*

liv - eth a - gain! Christ hath a - risen! He lives no more to die;
once Je - sus lay. Christ hath a - risen! etc.
deem - er to be. Christ hath a - risen! etc.
greet His re - turn. Christ hath a - risen! etc.

Copyright, 1891, by P. Bilhorn.

Christ Hath Arisen. Concluded.

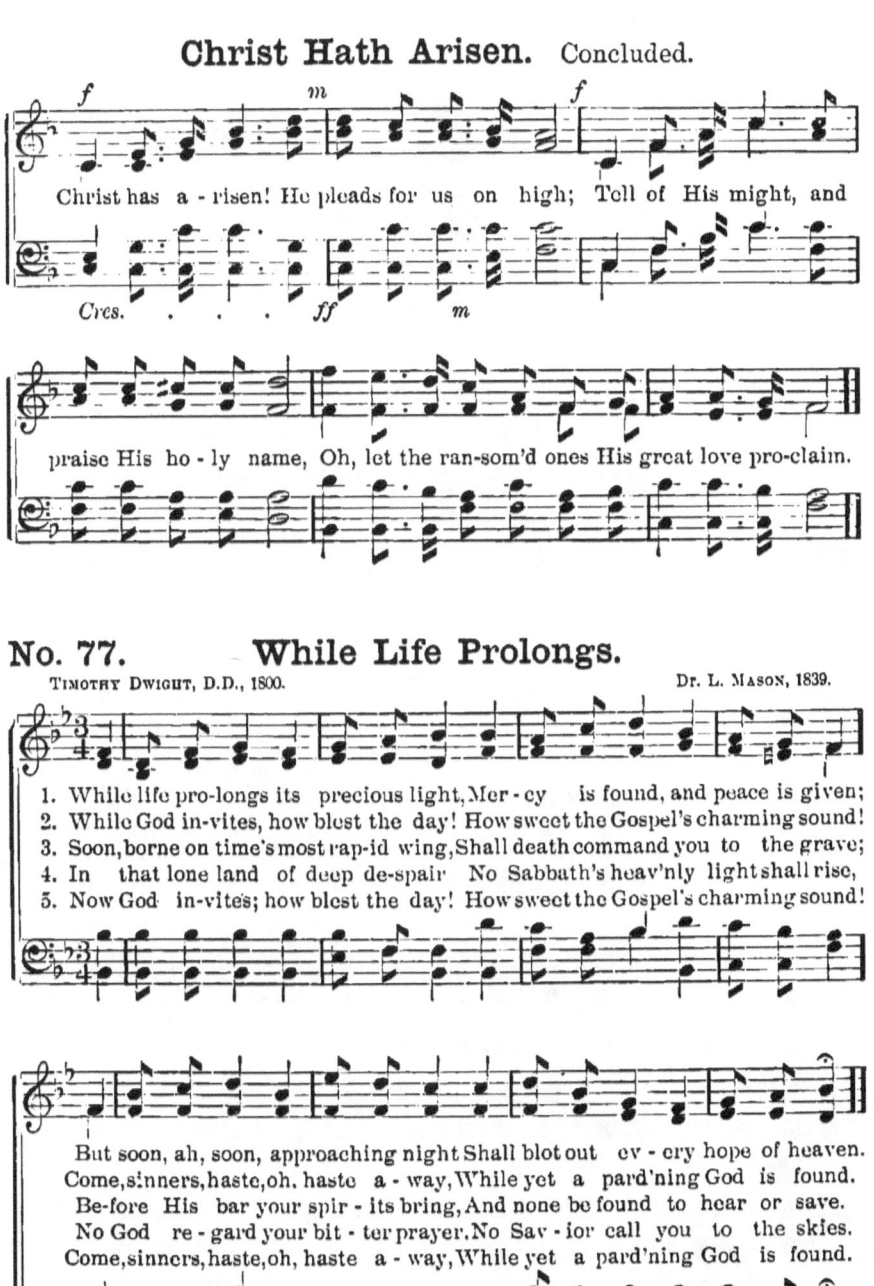

Christ has a-risen! He pleads for us on high; Tell of His might, and praise His ho-ly name, Oh, let the ran-som'd ones His great love pro-claim.

No. 77. While Life Prolongs.

TIMOTHY DWIGHT, D.D., 1800.

Dr. L. MASON, 1839.

1. While life pro-longs its precious light, Mer-cy is found, and peace is given;
2. While God in-vites, how blest the day! How sweet the Gospel's charming sound!
3. Soon, borne on time's most rap-id wing, Shall death command you to the grave;
4. In that lone land of deep de-spair No Sabbath's heav'nly light shall rise,
5. Now God in-vites; how blest the day! How sweet the Gospel's charming sound!

But soon, ah, soon, approaching night Shall blot out ev-ery hope of heaven.
Come, sinners, haste, oh, haste a-way, While yet a pard'ning God is found.
Be-fore His bar your spir-its bring, And none be found to hear or save.
No God re-gard your bit-ter prayer, No Sav-ior call you to the skies.
Come, sinners, haste, oh, haste a-way, While yet a pard'ning God is found.

No. 78. We Shall Triumph.

LAURA E NEWELL.

C. E. LESLIE.

1. Hark! I hear a shout a - long the line; Christ is lead - ing
2. We shall tri - umph in His glo-rious might; We will keep our
3. He, our For - tress, is our sure re - ward; We shall tri - umph,

with His love di - vine; "On, ye Chris-tian sol-diers, brave and true!"
gos - pel ar - mor bright; "On," He calls, "on, on to vic - to - ry!"
guid - ed by His word; Sound His or - der all a - long the line!

CHORUS.

This com - mand is giv'n to me and you.
Rise! take up your cross and fol - low me."
Christ, the bless - ed Lord doth bid us shine.
Christ is lead-ing this

might-y ar - my on; We shall tri-umph o - ver sin and wrong, Each re-

cruit has the ar-mor of the Lord, It is tak-en from His precious word.

By per.

No. 79. Believe and be Saved.

Miss ADA BLENKHORN.   P. BILHORN.

1. The voice of thy con-science oft whis-pers, Be-lieve on the
2. A voice in com-pas-sion is cry-ing, Be-lieve on the
3. God's voice and His good-ness are call-ing, Be-lieve on the
4. The voice of the Spir-it is plead-ing, Be-lieve on the

Lord and be saved, And turn from the path of trans-gres-sors; Be-
Lord and be saved, And cease from your sor-row and sigh-ing; Be-
Lord and be saved; The judg-ment of death is ap-pall-ing; Be-
Lord and be saved, While loved ones are now in-ter-ced-ing, Be-

lieve on the Lord and be saved. Be saved, (be saved,) be saved, (be saved,)

Be-lieve on the Lord and be saved, Be saved, (be saved,) be

saved, (be saved), Be-lieve on the Lord and be saved. (be saved).

No. 80. I've Been Redeemed.

F. M. D.

FRANK M. DAVIS.

1. All glo-ry to Je-sus, the ris-en Lord, Who re-
2. All glo-ry to Je-sus, my Sav-ior King, Who has
3. All glo-ry to Je-sus, the Prince of peace, He has

deemed me from my sin; Has spok-en His peace to my
shed His blood for me; He saw how my soul was in
filled my soul with joy; With rapt-ure I tell of His

CHORUS.

wea-ry soul, I am cleansed without, with-in.
bond-age held, And His mer-cy set me free. } I've been redeemed, I've
love a-broad, And His name's my sweet em-ploy.

been re-deemed, Been washed in the blood of the Lamb, (the Lamb,) I've

Repeat.

been re-deemed, I've been re-deemed, Been washed in the blood of the Lamb.

No. 81. Salvation is Free for All.

"Behold, now is the day of salvation."— 2 Cor. 6: 2.
"Whosoever will, let him take the water of life freely." — Rev. 22: 17.

P. B.

P. BILHORN.

1. Oh, ye who are bound by the fet-ters of sin, The Sav-iour has
2. Oh, come to the Sav-iour so lov-ing and kind, He bids ev-ery
3. Oh, how I re-joice since this Je-sus is mine, And His I for-
4. Oh, broth-er, the Sav-iour is call-ing thee now; From sin and its

pow'r to set free! He bled, and He died, on the cross cru-ci-fied, To
sor-row to cease! He bears ev-'ry grief, and He giv-eth re-lief: Sal-
ev-er shall be! His love I'll pro-claim, and I'll praise His dear name, Still
bond-age be free; There's pow'r in His name, if the prom-ise you'll claim: Sal-

CHORUS.

pur-chase sal-va-tion for thee! Sal-va-tion is free for
va-tion is com-fort and peace! Sal-va-tion, etc.
sing-ing, "Sal-va-tion is free!" Sal-va-tion, etc.
va-tion is wait-ing for thee! Sal-va-tion, etc.

you and for me; Oh, list to His gra-cious call! Sal-

va-tion is free for you and for me, Sal-va-tion is free for all.

No. 82.   Everlasting Life.

W. A. O.

W. A. Ogden.

1. Hear the prom-ise of the Lord, As re-cord-ed in His word,
2. Lit-tle chil-dren on the road To the cit-y of our God,
3. Cast on Him your load of care, Je-sus will your bur-den bear,

"Un-to you is ev-er-last-ing life!" Heav-y-la-den and distress'd,
"Un-to you is ev-er-last-ing life!" If on Je-sus you be-lieve,
"Un-to you is ev-er-last-ing life!" In the straight and narrow way

Come and I will give you rest, "Un-to you is ev-er-last-ing life!"
And His bless-ed word re-ceive, "Un-to you is ev-er-last-ing life!"
He will lead you day by day! "Un-to you is ev-er-last-ing life!"

CHORUS.

"Ev-er-last-ing life," the promise reads, While at God's right hand the Savior pleads;

Will you come to-day, making Christ your stay? For with Him is ev-er-last-ing life.

By permission.

No. 83. The Tidal Wave is Coming.

Rev. John P. Brooks.   L. White.

1. "The ti - dal wave is com - ing, sal - va - tion full and free,
2. "We're wait - ing, Lord, and long - ing, till Thou shalt come a - gain,
3. There's cleans - ing of - fered free - ly to all who come to - day,

With shout and song it sweeps a - long like bil - lows of the sea;
To claim Thine own, and on Thy throne, in peace and love to reign;
And trust - ing in the prom - is - es, will walk the nar - row way;

The ju - bi - lee of ho - li ness will ring thro' earth and sky, The dawn of
We'll wait that glorious com - ing till from out the op'-ning sky Our Lord shall
For per - fect peace in Him is found, and joys which ne'er shall die, And when He

D.S. *We'll wait that glorious mo - ment when from out the op'-ning sky, Our Lord shall*

FINE. CHORUS.

grace draws on a - pace, 'tis com - ing by and by.)
come to take us home, He's com - ing by and by. } Coming by and by,
comes we'll reign with Him, He's com - ing by and by.)

come to take us home—He's com-ing by and by.

D. S.

Coming by and by, A better day is dawning soon, He's coming by and by;

By permission.

No. 84. Singing as We Journey to Zion.

ADA BLENKHORN.

P. BILHORN.

1. We'll watch and pray and la-bor ev-'ry day, Sing-ing as we jour-ney to Zi - on, Till He shall come to call His chil-dren home,
2. With Christ as guide no e - vil can be - tide, Sing-ing as we jour-ney to Zi - on, We'll trust His grace till we be - hold His face,
3. With shield and sword we'll bat - tle for the Lord, Sing-ing as we jour-ney to Zi - on, We'll trust our King us vic - to - ry to bring,
4. The vic - t'ry won, we'll glo - ri - fy the Son, Sing-ing as we jour-ney to Zi - on, The "blood-wash'd throng" will wel-come us ere long,

Sing-ing as we jour - ney to Zi - on. Look - ing to our Lord, trust-ing in His word, March-ing when He bids us go for-ward;
Sing-ing as we jour - ney to Zi - on. Love with - in our heart, bids all fear de - part, Win - ning oth - er souls for the Mas - ter;
Sing-ing as we jour - ney to Zi - on. Striv - ing for the right, put - ting foes to flight, Fol - low - ing our Guide where He leads us;
Sing-ing as we jour - ney to Zi - on. Read - y! be our cry, when the Lord is nigh, Call - ing us to lay down our ar - mor;

Singing as We Journey to Zion. Concluded.

By His strong hand we'll pass the Canaan land, Singing as we journey to Zi - on.
He's al - ways near our pilgrim way to cheer, Singing as we journey to Zi - on.
By His great might we'll conquer in the fight, Singing as we journey to Zi - on.
Our war-fare, past we'll gather home at last, Singing as we journey to Zi - on.

No. 85. Where will You Spend Eternity?

Rev. E. A. Hoffman.   J. H. Tenney.

1. Where will you spend e - ter - ni - ty? This question comes to you and me!
2. Ma - ny are choosing Christ to - day, Turning from all their sins a - way;
3. Leav-ing the strait and nar-row way, Go - ing the downward road to - day,
4. Re - pent, be-lieve, this ver - y hour, Trust in the Sav - ior's grace and pow'r,

Tell me, what shall your an-swer be? Where will you spend e - ter - ni - ty?
Heav'n shall their hap - py por-tion be, Where will you spend e - ter - ni - ty?
Sad will their fi - nal end-ing be,—Lost thro' a long e - ter - ni - ty!
Then will your joy - ous an-swer be, Saved thro' a long e - ter - ni - ty!

REFRAIN.

E - ter - ni - ty! e - ter - ni - ty! Where will you spend e - ter - ni - ty?
3d v. E - ter - ni - ty! e - ter - ni - ty! Lost thro' a long e - ter - ni - ty!
4th v. E - ter - ni - ty! e - ter - ni - ty! Saved thro' a long e - ter - ni - ty!

No. 86. Tell it Again.

Mrs. Mary B. C. Slade.   R. M. McIntosh.

1. In - to the tent where a gyp - sy boy lay, Dy - ing a - lone at the
2. "Did He so love me, a poor lit - tle boy? Send un - to me the good
3. Bending, we caught the last words of his breath, Just as he en - tered the
4. Smil-ing, he said, as his last sigh was spent, "I am so glad that for

close of the day, News of sal - va - tion we car - ried, said he,
ti - dings of joy? Need I not per - ish? my hand will He hold?
val - ley of death: "God sent His Son:—who - so - ev - er!" said he;
me He was sent!" Whispered, while low sank the sun in the west,

CHORUS.

"No - bod - y ev - er has told it to me."
No - bod - y ev - er the sto - ry has told."
"Then I am sure that He sent Him for me"
"Lord, I be - lieve! tell it now to the rest."
Tell it a - gain! Tell it a - gain!

Sal - va - tion's sto - ry re - peat o'er and o'er, Till none can say of the

chil - dren of men, No - bod - y ev - er has told me be - fore.

No. 87. Glad Tidings of Joy.

W. A. O.

W. A. OGDEN. By per.

1. O Zi - on that bring-est good tid - ings, Lift up your glad
2. O Zi - on that bring-est good tid - ings, The Bride-groom is
3. O Zi - on that bring-est good tid - ings, The hope of the

voice to the skies, Go pub - lish sal - va - tion thro' Je - sus,
com - ing this way, Go forth in thy splen - dor to meet Him,
world is in thee, Pro-claim to the sin - ner sal - va - tion,

CHORUS.

Bid na-tions from darkness a rise. Go tell............ the glad
A - rise in thy beau - ty to - day. Go tell the glad tid-ings, glad
And bid him from bond-age go free.

tid - - - ings, The won - - - - der-ful tid - - - ings, Glad
tid-ings of joy, The won-der - ful, won-der - ful tid - ings of joy,

tid-ings of joy, Glad tidings of joy, Go tell the glad tidings of joy......
of joy.

No. 88.   Look Away to Jesus.

JULIA H. JOHNSTON.   A. BEIRLY. By per.

Spirited.

1. Is thy heart de-filed with-in, Is thy guilt ap-pall-ing?
2. In the hour of pain and fear, When thy foes o'er-take thee,
3. In the sun-shine and the night, In thy joy or sad-ness,
4. All our sins He bore a-lone, But, when we be-lieve it,

Look a-way from self and sin, Hear thy Sav-ior call-ing.
Look to Je-sus, He is near, He will not for-sake thee.
Look to Je-sus Christ the light, He will bring thee glad-ness.
He will share His peace un-known, If we will re-ceive it.

'Tis the voice of love and might, Ten-der-ly ap-peal-ing,
Earth-ly help-ers faint and fall, Je-sus fail-eth nev-er,
From thy bur-den turn thy face, He can well sus-tain thee,
Turn from joys of world-ly birth, Fit-ful-ly al-lur-ing,

"Find in me thy life and light, I will bring thee heal-ing."
In His name shalt thou pre-vail, Trust in Him for-ev-er.
In thy glad-ness, seek His grace, Let His love con-strain thee.
Look to things of high-er worth, Ev-er-more en-dur-ing.

Look Away to Jesus. Concluded.

CHORUS.

Look a - way (look a-way) from self and sin, Look a - way (look a-way) to

Je-sus, Let Him reign su-preme with-in, Look a-way (look a-way) to Je - sus.

Rit.

No. 89.   A Charge to Keep I Have.

Rev. CHAS. WESLEY.   Dr. LOWELL MASON.

1. A charge to keep I have, A God to glo - ri - fy;
2. To serve the pres - ent age, My call - ing to ful - fill;
3. Arm me with jeal - ous care, As in Thy sight to live;
4. Help me to watch and pray, And on Thy - self re - ly;

A nev-er - dy-ing soul to save, And fit it for the sky.
Oh, may it all my powers en - gage, To do my Mas - ter's will.
And oh, Thy ser- vant, Lord! pre - pare, A strict ac - count to give.
As-sured if I my trust be - tray, I shall for - ev - er die.

No. 90. Christ will Welcome Thee.

Miss A. Smith. P. Bilhorn.

1. I heard of Je-sus, the Sav-ior, So ten-der, lov-ing and kind,
2. I came to Je-sus, my Sav-ior, And found sweet peace to my soul;
3. And now with Je-sus, my Sav-ior, I walk each day hand in hand,
4. Oh, come to Je-sus, my Sav-ior, You'll find His prom-is-es true;

That those who seek for His fa-vor Rich bless-ings sure-ly may find.
Tho' sin-ful, wretch-ed and wea-ry, He bade me quick-ly be whole.
All need-ed grac-es He gives me, And strength each mo-ment to stand.
And trusting Him midst temptation, He'll safe-ly car-ry you through.

REFRAIN.

For Christ will welcome the sin-ner, Tho' vile so-ev-er he be;

Then come this mo-ment and prove Him, He of-fers par-don to thee.

No. 91.   Walk in the Light.

BERNARD BARTON.   Rev. J. H. WELCH.

1. Walk in the light! so shalt thou know That fel-low-ship of love,
2. Walk in the light! and thou shalt own Thy darkness passed a-way,
3. Walk in the light! and e'en the tomb No fear-ful shade shall wear;
4. Walk in the light! and thine shall be A path, tho' thorn-y, bright;

His Spir-it on-ly can be-stow Who reigns in light a-bove.
Be-cause that light on thee hath shone In which is per-fect day.
Glo-ry shall chase a-way its gloom, For Christ hath conquerd there.
For God, by grace, shall dwell in thee, And God Him-self is light.

CHORUS.

We'll walk.......... in the light,.......... In the

We'll walk in the light, in the beau-ti-ful light, In the

beau - - ti-ful light;........ We'll walk.......... in the

won-der-ful light, in the light of our God; We'll walk in the light, in the

light........ In the light.......... of our God..........

beau-ti-ful light, In the won-der-ful light, in the light of our God.

No. 92. Who Will Go?

Rev. D. March. P. Bilhorn.

1. Hark! the voice of Je-sus cry-ing, "Who will go and work to-day?
2. If you can-not cross the o-cean, And the heath-en lands ex-plore,
3. If you can-not speak like an-gels, If you can-not preach like Paul,
4. If a-mong the old-er peo-ple, You may not be apt to teach;
5. Let none hear you i-dly say-ing, "There is noth-ing I can do,"

Fields are white and har-vest wait-ing, Who will bear the sheaves a-way?"
You can find the heath-en near-er, You can help them at your door.
You can tell the love of Je-sus, You can say He died for all.
"Feed my Lambs," said Christ, our Shepherd, "Place the food with-in our reach."
While the souls of men are dy-ing, And the Mas-ter calls for you.

Loud and strong the Mas-ter call-eth, Rich re-ward He of-fers thee:
If you can-not give your thousands, You can give the wid-ow's mite.
If you can-not rouse the wick-ed With the judgment's dread a-larms,
And it may be that the chil-dren You have led with trembling hand,
Take the task He gives you glad-ly, Let His work your pleas-ure be;

Who will an-swer, glad-ly say-ing, "Here am I; send me, send me?"
And the least you do for Je-sus, Will be pre-cious in His sight.
You can lead the lit-tle chil-dren To the Sav-ior's wait-ing arms.
Will be found a-mong your jew-els, When you reach the bet-ter land.
An-swer quick-ly when He call-eth, "Here am I; send me, send me!"

Copyright, 1891, by P. Bilhorn.

No. 93. There Stood a Cross.

Rev. E. A. Hoffman.   Rev. J. H. Welch.

Slow.

1. On Cal - va - ry there stood a Cross, And nailed there-on was One
2. There the Re-deem - er gave His blood To ran - som me from sin,
3. Up - on that Cross, that bit - ter Cross, My weight of guilt He bore,
4. Be - fore that Cross I weep and pray, And wor - ship and a - dore,

Who was the bear - er of my sin, God's well - be - lov - ed Son.
And made an end of all my guilt, And brought re - demp-tion in.
So - cured a clear-ance for my sins; My soul can ask no more.
And God's free grace I will ex - tol And laud for ev - er-more.

CHORUS.

Oh, the blood of the Lamb! Oh, the blood of the Lamb,

That was shed on Cal - va - ry! It was shed for you,

It was shed for me, When He died up - on the tree.

No. 94. Meet Me There.

Henrietta E. Blair.   Wm. J. Kirkpatrick. By per.

1. On the hap-py, gold-en shore, Where the faith-ful part no more, When the
2. Here our fond-est hopes are vain, Dear-est links are rent in twain; But in
3. Where the harps of an-gels ring, And the blest for-ev-er sing, In the

storms of life are o'er, Meet me there; Where the night dissolves a-way In-to
heav'n no throb of pain, Meet me there; By the riv-er sparkling bright, In the
pal-ace of the King, Meet me there; Where in sweet communion blend Heart with

FINE.

pure and per-fect day, I am go-ing home to stay, Meet me there.
cit-y of de-light, Where our faith is lost in sight, Meet me there.
heart, and friend with friend, In a world that ne'er shall end, Meet me there.

D. S. hap-py, gold-en shore, Where the faith-ful part no more, Meet me there.

CHORUS.

Meet me there,   Meet me there,   Where the tree of life is
Meet me there,   Meet me there,

D. S.

blooming, Meet me there,   When the storms of life are o'er, On the
Meet me there,

Love Divine.

CHAS. WESLEY.   JOHN ZUNDEL.

1. Love di - vine, all love ex - cell - ing, Joy of heav'n, to earth come down!
2. Breathe, O breathe Thy lov - ing Spir - it In - to ev - 'ry troub - led breast!
3. Come, Al - might - y to de - liv - er, Let us all Thy life re - ceive;
4. Fin - ish then Thy new cre - a - tion; Pure and spot - less let us be;

Fix in us Thy hum - ble dwelling; All Thy faith - ful mer - cies crown.
Let us all in Thee in - her - it, Let us find that sec - ond rest.
Sud - den - ly re - turn, and nev - er, Nev - er more Thy tem - ples leave:
Let us see Thy great sal - va - tion, Per - fect - ly re - stored in Thee:

Je - sus, Thou art all compas - sion, Pure, un - bound - ed love Thou art;
Take a - way our bent to sin - ning; Al - pha and O - me - ga be;
Thee we would be al - ways blessing, Serve Thee as Thy hosts a - bove,
Changed from glo - ry in - to glo - ry, Till in heav'n we take our place,

Vis - it us with Thy sal - va - tion; En - ter ev - 'ry trembling heart.
End of faith, as its be - gin - ning, Set our hearts at lib - er - ty.
Pray and praise Thee with - out ceas - ing, Glo - ry in Thy per - fect love.
Till we cast our crowns be - fore Thee: Lost in won - der, love, and praise.

No. 96. O Beautiful Home.

ADA BLENKHORN

P. BILHORN.

1. O beau-ti-ful home in glo - ry, Near to the crys-tal sea,
2. O beau-ti-ful home where an - gels, Clad in their robes of white,
3. O beau-ti-ful home where loved ones Hun-ger and thirst no more,
4. O beau-ti-ful home where Je - sus Wait-eth to wel-come me,

Where fountains of liv-ing wa-ter Flow-ing for-ev-er free;
In tem-ple of gold and jas-per, Serve Him both day and night:
For Je-sus him-self doth lead them Safe on that hap-py shore.
I long to be-hold its splen-dor, Ev-er with Him to be.

There doth our dear Re-deem-er For us pre-pare a place,
"Hon-or, and might, and pow-er, Be to the Lamb once slain—
There by the crys-tal riv-er, Where grows the "tree of life,"
Glad-ly my ran-somed spir-it Home-ward would take its flight,

That thro' the bless-ed For-ev-er We may be-hold His face.
Glo-ry to God in the high-est!" Is their tri-umph-ant strain.
Sweet is the rapt-ur-ous glo-ry, Blest is the end-ed strife.
Dwell with the loved in His pres-ence, Rest in e-ter-nal light.

No. 97.   I'm Thine, Forever Thine.

WARREN W. BENTLEY.

1. No more my own, Lord Je - sus, Bought with Thy pre - cious blood;
2. I give the life Thou gav - est, My pres - ent, fu - ture, past,
3. I give the love, the sweet-est Thy good-ness grants to me;
4. Out - side the camp to suf -fer, With - in the vale to meet;

I give Thee but Thine own, Lord, That long Thy love with-stood.
My joys, my fears, my sor - rows, My first hope and my last.
Oh, take and make it meet, Lord, For of - fer - ing to Thee.
And hear the soft - est whis - per, From out the mer - cy - seat.

CHORUS.

Now fash - ion, form, and fill me With light and love di - vine;

So, one with Thee, Lord, Je - sus, I'm Thine, for - ev - er Thine.

No. 98.   Come to the Feast.

W. A. O.

W. A. Ogden. By per.

1. Come to the feast, that the Lord hath spread, Here ev - 'ry soul may be
2. Come to the feast, leave your care and strife, Come, for His word is with
3. Come to the feast, hear the gos - pel word, Come while your heart by its

tru - ly fed; Come in the name of the Liv - ing Head,
bless - ing rife; For un - to you is e - ter - nal life,
pow'r is stirred; Fly to the ark like the wea - ry bird,

CHORUS.

Washed in the blood of the Lamb. Washed in the blood of the

Lamb, (the Lamb), Washed in the blood of the Lamb; Come and your soul

shall be tru - ly fed, Washed in the blood of the Lamb.

Copyright, 1891, by W. A. Ogden.

No. 99. Over Jordan.

F. A. B.

F. A. BLACKMER.

1. In that coun-try which lies o - ver Jor - dan, In that
2. O - ver there are the beau-ti - ful man - sions That the
3. All the dear ones we lov'd, and who lov'd us, We shall
4. We shall there see the face of the Fa - ther, Who for

sweet Par - a - dise o - ver there, We are go - ing to dwell
Sav - ior has gone to pre - pare, And the cit - y of God,
meet on that sor - row - less shore, Glo - ri - fied, made im - mor-
mor - tals such won - ders has done; Who to die for us while

CHORUS.

with the Sav - ior, And with Him end-less glo - ry share.
bright and gold - en, With its walls deck'd with jewels rare.
tal and tear - less; We shall meet there to part no more.
we were reb - els, Sent His on - ly be - got - ten Son.

O - ver
Jor-dan, O - ver Jor - dan, In that sweet Par - a - dise o - ver there, We are

go - ing to dwell with the Sav - ior, And with Him end-less glory share.

No. 100. Because He so Loves Me.

D. Y. B.

Rev. D. Y. BAGBY, Ph. D.

DUET.

1. Why am I so hap-py and free from all sin? Be-cause my dear
2. When I was a sin-ner why was I His choice? Be-cause my dear
3. And still I re-joice, when much old-er I'm grown, Be-cause my dear

Sav-ior so loves me. Why do I re-joice and am hap-py with-in?
Sav-ior so loved me. When I'm in af-flic-tion, why do I re-joice?
Sav-ior so loves me. My poor heart re-joic-es with pleasures un-known,

SEMI CHORUS.

Be-cause my dear Sav-ior so loves me. 'Tis Je-sus, my Sav-ior, all

REFRAIN.

blessings bestows; 'Tis Je-sus relieves me from all of my woes, My sins He for-

gives, for my weakness He knows, Because my dear Savior so loves me.

Come to Jesus.

E. R. Latta.   J. H. Tenney. By per.

1 Come to Je - sus! He will save you, Tho' your sins as crim-son glow;
2 Come to Je - sus! do not tar - ry; En - ter in at mer-cy's gate;
3 Come to Je - sus, dy - ing sin - ner! Oth - er Sav-ior there is none;

If you give your hearts to Je - sus, He will make them white as snow.
Oh, de - lay not till the mor-row, Lest thy com-ing be too late.
He will share with you His glo - ry, When your pil-grim-age is done.

CHORUS.

Come to Je - - - - sus! Come to Je - - - - sus! Come to
Come, come to-day!   Come, come to-day! Come to

Je - sus! come to - day!   Come to Je - - - - sus!
Je - sus! come, yes, come, come to - day!   Come, come to - day!

Come to Je - - - - sus! Come to Je - sus! come, come to-day!
Come, come to-day!

No. 102. The Years are Rolling on.

HARRIET B. McKEEVER. JNO. R. SWENEY.

Recitante.

1. In a world so full of weep-ing, While the years are roll-ing on,
2. There's no time to waste in sigh-ing, While the years are roll-ing on;
3. Let us strengthen one an-oth-er, While the years are roll-ing on;
4. Friends we love are quick-ly fly-ing, While the years are roll-ing on;

Christian souls the watch are keep-ing, While the years are roll-ing on.
Time is fly-ing, souls are dy-ing, While the years are roll-ing on.
Seek to raise a fall-en broth-er, While the years are roll-ing on.
No more part-ing, no more dy-ing, While the years are roll-ing on.

While our jour-ney we pur-sue, With the ha-ven still in view,
Lov-ing words a soul may win, From the wretch-ed paths of sin;
This is work for ev-'ry hand, Till, throughout cre-a-tion's land,
In the world be-yond the tomb Sor-row nev-er more can come,

There is work for us to do, While the years are roll-ing on.
We may bring the wan-d'rers in, While the years are roll-ing on.
Ar-mies for the Lord shall stand, While the years are roll-ing on.
When we meet in that blest home, While the years are roll-ing on.

CHORUS.

Are roll-ing on, are roll-ing on, Are roll-ing on, are roll-ing on,

The Years are Rolling on. Concluded.

Oh, the joy that we may scat-ter, While the years are roll-ing on.

No. 103.   Hosanna! Hosanna!

Rev. J. H. Weber.   Rev. J. H. Weber.

1. I've found a glad ho-san-na, It's glo-ry in my soul!
2. I've found a glad ho-san-na, A balm for ev-'ry woe;
3. I've found a glad ho-san-na, That gives my poor heart rest;

I can not keep from sing-ing, For Je-sus makes me whole.
The blood of Christ it wash-es, And makes me white as snow!
For Je-sus dwells with-in me, And I am tru-ly blest!

CHORUS.

Ho-san-na! ho-san-na! Prais-es to our King!

Ho-san-na! ho-san-na, To Je-sus will I sing.

No. 104.   Waiting for the Savior.

Rev. G. W. Crofts.

P. Bilhorn.

1. We are wait-ing for the Sav-ior, As the watch-er waits the light,
2. We are wait-ing for the Sav-ior, For our hearts are sick of sin,
3. We are wait-ing for the Sav-ior, In our sor-row and our grief,
4. We are wait-ing for the Sav-ior, For the night comes on a-pace;

When the sun in all his glo-ry Drives a-way the shades of night;
And there's no one here to heal us Of the pain we feel with-in;
Wait-ing for the great Con-sol-er, Who will bring a sweet re-lief;
Long-er grow the som-ber shad-ows 'Round our earth-ly dwell-ing-place,

We are wait-ing, on-ly wait-ing, For the Mas-ter to ap-pear,
There is no one but the Sav-ior, Who can cleanse the guilt-y soul,
Who will give for all our mourning, Oil of His a-bound-ing joy;
Soon we'll take the hap-py jour-ney, On the bright and shin-ing sea:

On-ly wait-ing for His pres-ence Full of com-fort and of cheer.
Take a-way the troubled con-science, Make the bro-ken spir-it whole.
For our heav-i-ness of spir-it, Songs of praise the saints em-ploy.
And how glad-ly, bless-ed Sav-ior, Since we wait to sail with Thee.

Waiting for the Savior. Concluded.

CHORUS.

We are wait - - ing, We are watch - - ing,
We are wait - ing for our Sav - ior, We are watch-ing for our King,

We are read - y for the Mas - ter to ap - pear, (to ap - pear,)

We are wait - - ing, We are watch - - ing
We are wait - ing for our Sav - ior, We are watch - ing for our King,

For the com - ing of our Lord is draw-ing near, (draw-ing near.)

No. 105. Christ, our Rock!

I Cor. 10: 4. Deut. 32: 31.

P. B.
Moderato.

P. Bilhorn.

1. When wea - ry and faint - - ing and read - y to
2. When thirst - y and parched with the heat...... of the
3. Though bil - lows of sor - row a - round...... me may

die,....... To the Rock...... in the des - ert for
day,...... To the Rock...... that was smit - ten I'll
roll, ... And dan - gers of mid - night may

safe - ty I fly;........ There, 'neath...... its cool
haste...... me and say,....... Give me........ a cool
troub - le my soul,....... I'll haste....... to the

Christ, our Rock! Concluded.

shel - ter from storms..... I would hide;...... My
drink...... from Thy boun - ti - ful store,..... And
Rock....... that is high - er than I,......... And

soul....... is re - freshed as in Him I a - bide.
quick - ly and free - ly the life wa - ters pour.
safe - ly I'll rest........ till the night pass - eth by.

CHORUS.

O come all ye wea - ry, And bliss - ful - ly prove

That Christ is the Rock, And His shad-ow is love.

No. 106. The Haven of Rest.

H. L. GILMOUR.   GEO. D. MOORE.

1. My soul in sad ex - ile was out on life's sea, So
2. I yield - ed my - self to His ten - der em - brace, And
3. The song of my soul, since the Lord made me whole, Has
4. Oh, come to the Sav - ior, He pa - tient-ly waits To

bur-dened with sin, and dis - tress, Till I heard a sweet voice say - ing,
faith tak - ing hold of the word, My fet - ters fell off, and I
been the OLD STO - RY so blest Of Je - sus, who'll save who-so-
save by His pow - er di - vine; Come, an - chor your soul in the

D. S. *The tem - pest may sweep o'er the*

FINE.

make me your choice; And I en-tered the "Ha - ven of Rest!"
an-chored my soul; The ha - ven of rest is my Lord.
ev - er will have A home in the "Ha - ven of Rest!"
ha - ven of rest, And say, "my Be - lov - ed is mine."

wild, storm - y deep, In Je - sus I'm safe ev - er - more.

CHORUS.   D. S.

I've anchor'd my soul in the ha-ven of rest, I'll sail the wide seas no more;

No. 107.   Ever Be Faithful.

E. A. H.   Rev. E. A. Hoffman.

1. Ev - er to Je - sus be faith - ful and true, He has been ten - der and
2. Hon - or the Mas - ter by do - ing His will, Love Him, and all His com-
3. Cling un - to Je - sus, thy Strength and thy Might, Cling in the dark - ness, and

faith - ful to you; Fol - low Him dai - ly what - ev - er be - tide,
mand-ments ful - fill; And as you jour - ney life's pil-grim - age through,
cling in the light, Hon - or His name in what - ev - er you do,

CHORUS.

Fol - low your Lead - er and Guide. Ev - - - - - er be
Ev - er be faith - ful and true.
Ev - er be faith - ful and true.   Ev - er be faith - ful and

faith - - - ful, Ev - - - - - - er be faith - - - ful,
ev - er be true, Ev - er be faith - ful and ev - er be true,

Ev - - - - - er be faith - - ful, Ev - - - er be true.
He has been ten - der and faithful to you, Ev - er be faithful and true.

No. 108. God Will Help You Stand.

Words suggested by the following incident: A young man, the only son of respectable parents, well educated, and with natural qualities which would enable him to do a great deal of good in the world, became addicted to the use of strong drink. He tried in his own strength again and again to reform, but without success. Every effort seemed a failure. Finally, he determined to end his miserable existence by drowning in Lake Michigan. But by the providence of God, he was met on the way by a Christian gentleman, who persuaded him to abandon his purpose, and accept Jesus, which he did.

L. W. Lyon.   P. Bilhorn.

1. Tho' the way seems dark be - fore you, Broth - er, don't de - spair;
2. Is your heart de - pressed, my broth - er? Je - sus is your friend;
3. At the hearth-stone lov'd ones pray - ing, Plead - ing for their son,
4. Ma - ny pray'rs for you are ris - ing To the throne of grace,

Bright - er light shall yet shine o'er you, In this world of care.
He will save you, He will lead you To your jour - ney's end.
With a par - ent's sup - pli - ca - tion For the way - ward one.
Can you still His love de - spis - ing, Turn from Him your face?

He who by His might - y pow - er, Holds the sea and land,
Do not fear to trust Him, broth - er, See His wound - ed hand;
Loved one, cast your sins be - hind you, Join the ran - somed band;
Broth - er, rise from sin and sor - row, Take thy Fa - ther's hand;

Still is near, tho' dark the hour, He will help you stand.
He has died for your re - demp - tion, He will help you stand.
Grace suf - fi - cient He will give you, He will help you stand.
Fear no doubt of sin to - mor - row, He will help you stand.

God Will Help You Stand. Concluded.

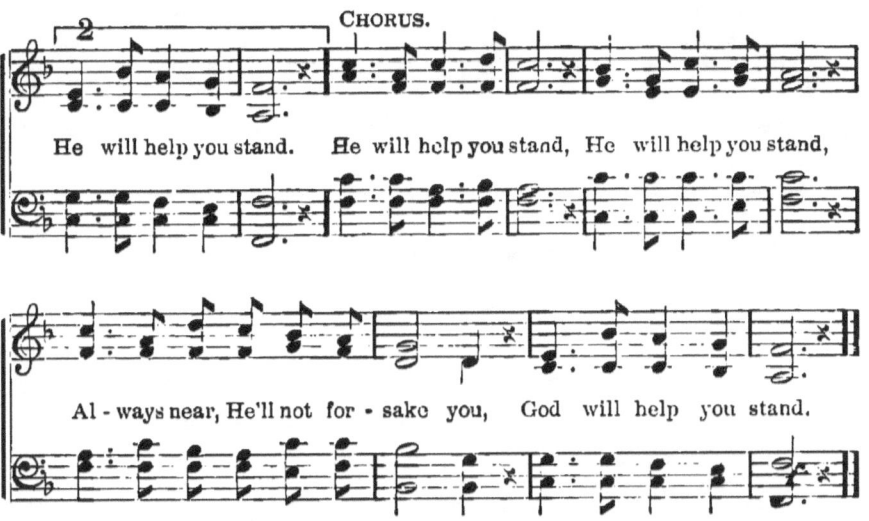

He will help you stand. He will help you stand, He will help you stand,

Al - ways near, He'll not for - sake you, God will help you stand.

No. 109. Only a Word for the Master.

C. E. P.   CHAS. EDW. POLLOCK. By per.

Slow, with pathos.

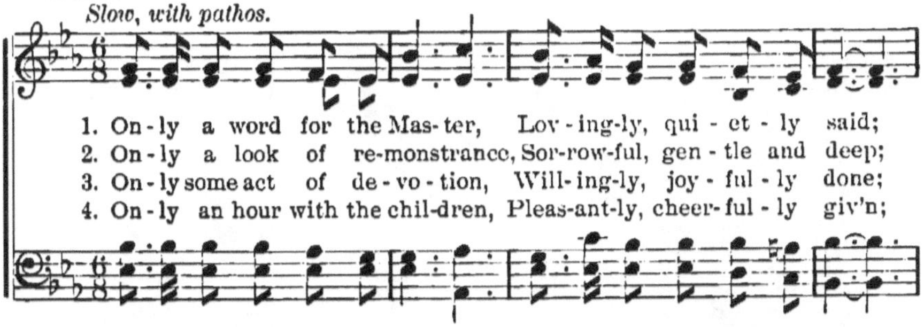

1. On - ly a word for the Mas - ter, Lov - ing - ly, qui - et - ly said;
2. On - ly a look of re - monstrance, Sor - row - ful, gen - tle and deep;
3. On - ly some act of de - vo - tion, Will - ing - ly, joy - ful - ly done;
4. On - ly an hour with the chil - dren, Pleas - ant - ly, cheer - ful - ly giv'n;

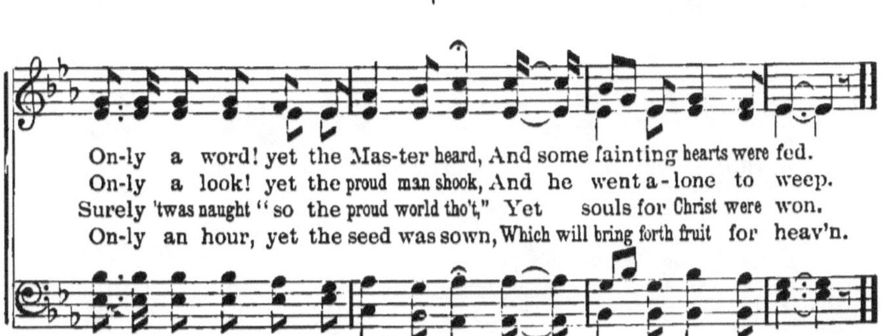

On - ly a word! yet the Mas - ter heard, And some fainting hearts were fed.
On - ly a look! yet the proud man shook, And he went a - lone to weep.
Surely 'twas naught "so the proud world tho't," Yet souls for Christ were won.
On - ly an hour, yet the seed was sown, Which will bring forth fruit for heav'n.

8

No. 110.   Decide To-Night.

Slow and with expression.   *Effective as a solo.*   W. A. SPENCER. By per.

1. Some go a-way from the house to-night,   Pu - ri - fied from sin;
2. Some will go out from the house to-night,   Har - den'd by de - lay,
3. Some will go out from the house to-night,   Full of trust in God,
4. Wait-ing a mo - ment more for thee,   Je - sus still en - treats;

CHORUS. *Go-ing a - way from Christ to-night, A-way from His lov - ing care;*

FINE.

Oth - ers re - ject the pre-cious light, And go a - way un - clean;
Yield-ing to sa - tan's lur - ing snare, Will hope-less turn a - way;
Hap - py in heart, made pure and white, By Je - sus' pre - cious blood;
Soon will the knocking end - ed be, That now thy closed heart beats,

Go - ing a - way from bless - ed light, To dark-ness and de - spair.

Lov - ing - ly still the Sav - ior stands, Plead-ing with thy heart;
Nev - er - more shall the Spir - it plead At the bolt - ed door;
Go not a - way, poor wan-d'rer stay Till thou too art free!
Stay, sin - ner, stay at Mer - cy's door, Seek the o - pen gate:

D. C.

Patiently knocks with His bleeding hands, Un - will - ing to de - part.
Now is the hour of thy soul's great need, 'Tis now or nev - er - more.
Walking with Christ life's hap-py way, Most bless - ed shalt thou be.
Sin-ner, de - cide, lest hope be o'er, And thou shouldst be too late.

No. 111. Footsteps of Jesus.

LIZZIE ASHBAUGH. GEO. J. KURZENKNABE.

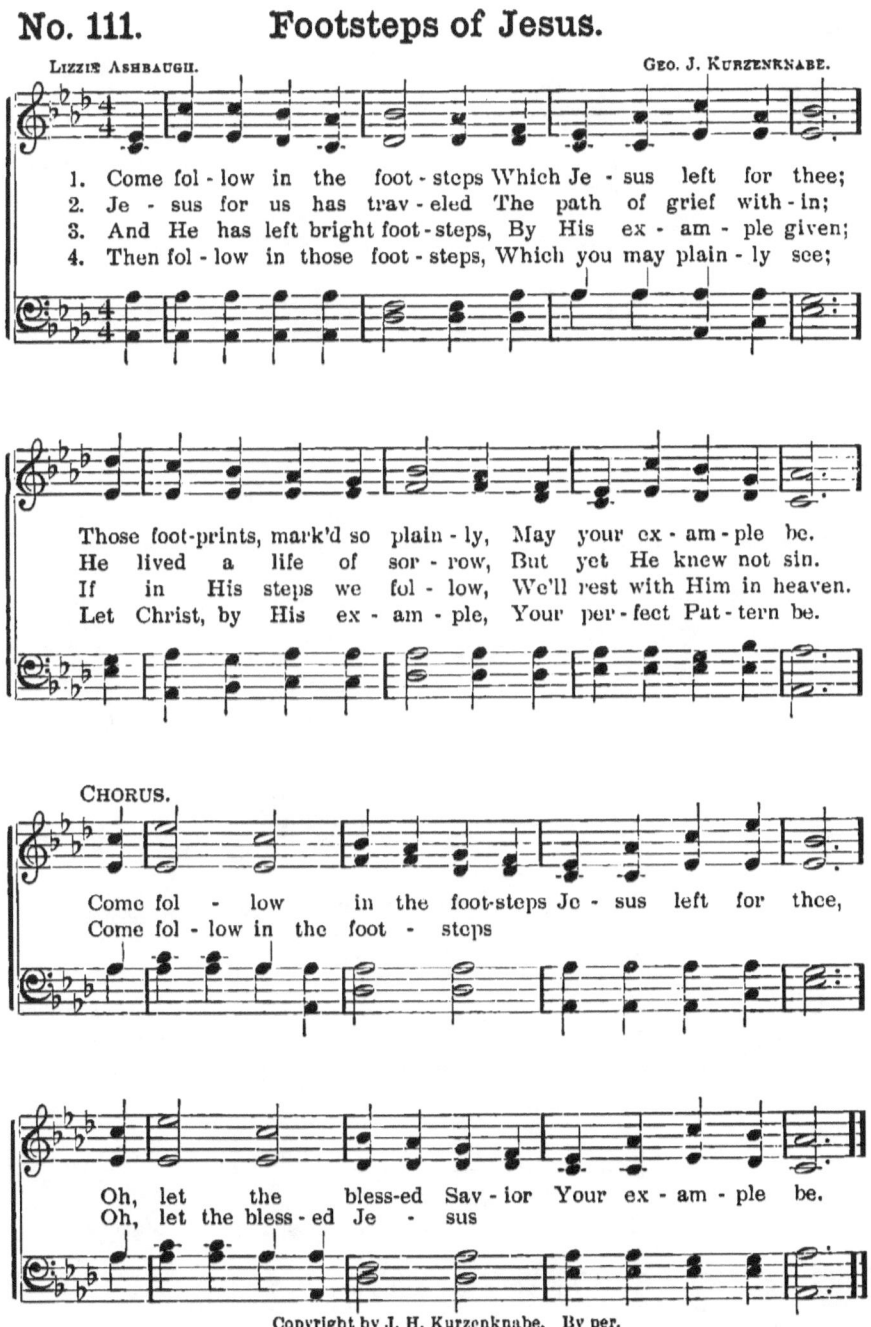

1. Come fol-low in the foot-steps Which Je-sus left for thee;
2. Je-sus for us has trav-eled The path of grief with-in;
3. And He has left bright foot-steps, By His ex-am-ple given;
4. Then fol-low in those foot-steps, Which you may plain-ly see;

Those foot-prints, mark'd so plain-ly, May your ex-am-ple be.
He lived a life of sor-row, But yet He knew not sin.
If in His steps we fol-low, We'll rest with Him in heaven.
Let Christ, by His ex-am-ple, Your per-fect Pat-tern be.

CHORUS.

Come fol-low in the foot-steps Je-sus left for thee,
Come fol-low in the foot-steps

Oh, let the bless-ed Sav-ior Your ex-am-ple be.
Oh, let the bless-ed Je-sus

My Redeemer Lives.

Arr. by M. G. P.   Arr. by Rev. M. G. PRESCOTT.

1. I know that my Re-deem-er lives, That He's pre-
2. I'm trust-ing Je-sus Christ for all, I know His
3. And now be-wil-dered at the thought, I stand and
4. I know that soon my Lord will come, I know He

D. C. For I am on-ly wait-ing here, To hear the

pared a home for me, And crowns of vic-to-ry He gives
blood a-tones for me, I'm list-'ning for the gen-tle call
won-der at His love, How He from heav'n to earth was brought
will not tar-ry long, I know He soon will call me home

summons, "child, come home," For I am on-ly wait-ing here,

FINE. CHORUS.

To those who would His chil-dren be.
To say, the Mas-ter wait-eth thee.
To die, that I might live a-bove.
To sing with joy the heav'n-ly song.

Then ask me not to

To hear the sum-mons, "child, come home."

D. C.

min-gle on A-mid the gay and thought-less throng,

No. 113. Blessed be the Name.

W. H. CLARK.

Arr. by WM. J. KIRKPATRICK.

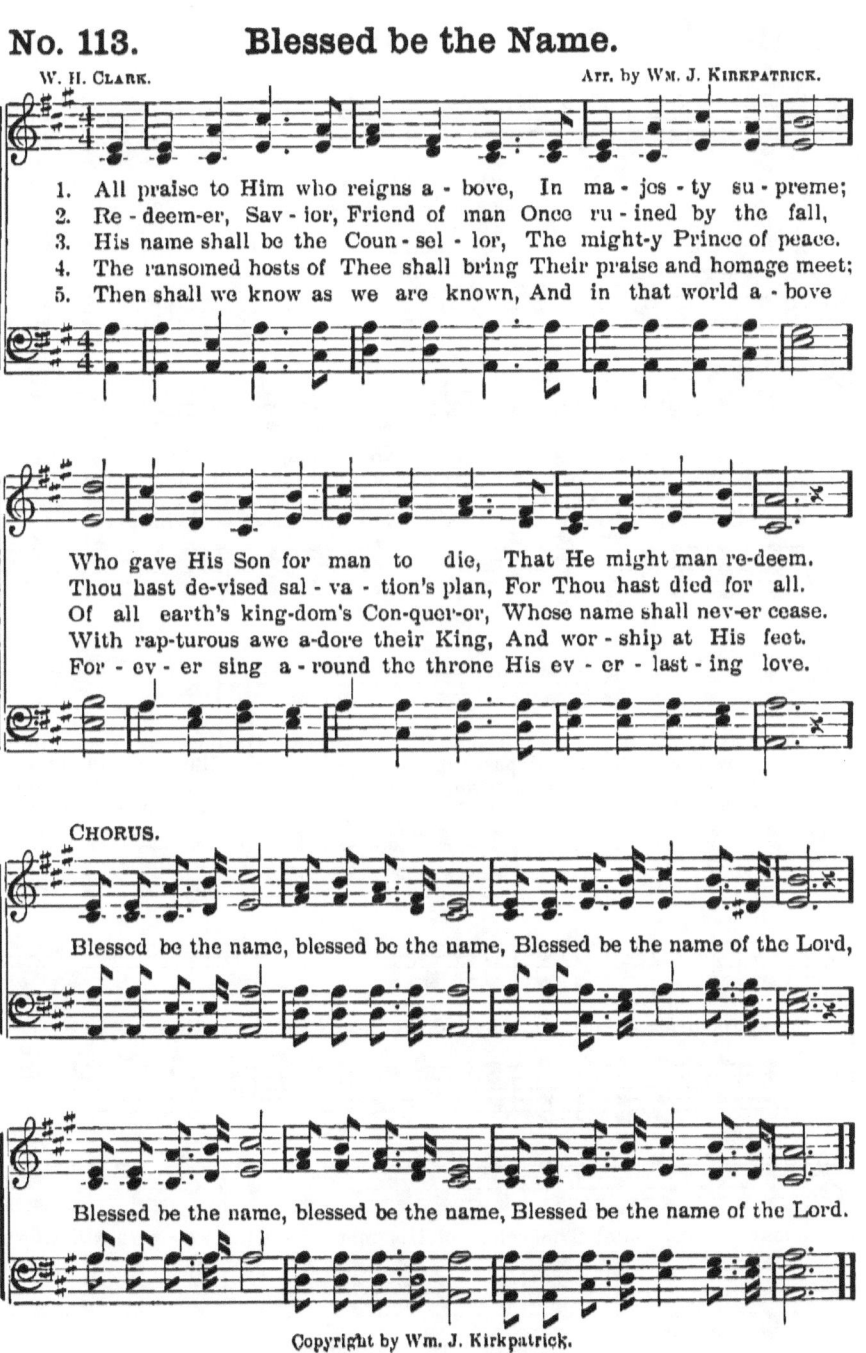

1. All praise to Him who reigns a - bove, In ma - jes - ty su - preme;
2. Re - deem-er, Sav - ior, Friend of man Once ru - ined by the fall,
3. His name shall be the Coun - sel - lor, The might-y Prince of peace.
4. The ransomed hosts of Thee shall bring Their praise and homage meet;
5. Then shall we know as we are known, And in that world a - bove

Who gave His Son for man to die, That He might man re-deem.
Thou hast de-vised sal - va - tion's plan, For Thou hast died for all.
Of all earth's king-dom's Con-quer-or, Whose name shall nev-er cease.
With rap-turous awe a-dore their King, And wor - ship at His feet.
For - ev - er sing a - round the throne His ev - er - last - ing love.

CHORUS.

Blessed be the name, blessed be the name, Blessed be the name of the Lord,

Blessed be the name, blessed be the name, Blessed be the name of the Lord.

No Room for Jesus.

Mrs. Hall.   P. Bilhorn.

1. No room for Je - sus! the world is so wide, Busi - ness and
2. No room for Je - sus! hearts bur - dened with care, Vain - ly seek
3. No room for Je - sus! when death is so near, Com - ing so
4. No room for Je - sus! oh, would I could tell, All of re-

pleas-ure thrust Je - sus a - side, No time to think of the
rest with-out 'e - ven a pray'r; And gleam-ing in fields that are
quick-ly, whose pres-ence we fear; When com - fort-less o - ver some
demp-tion so wise-ly and well, That some heart would hast - en to

heav - en so nigh, No room for Je - sus till just as you die.
bar - ren and dead, And pass-ing un - heed-ed the life - giv - ing bread.
loved one we weep, No room for Je - sus when sor - row runs deep.
o - pen the door, Make room for Je - sus to dwell ev - er-more.

CHORUS.

Make room for Je-sus, oh, why do you wait? If you thus tar - ry it

may be too late; The voice of His mer - cy death's wa - ters will drown,

Copyright, 1891, by P. Bilhorn.

No Room for Jesus. Concluded.

And you be too late for a king-dom, a crown.

H. G. SMEAD.   P. BILHORN.

No. 115.   Jesus, Redeemer.

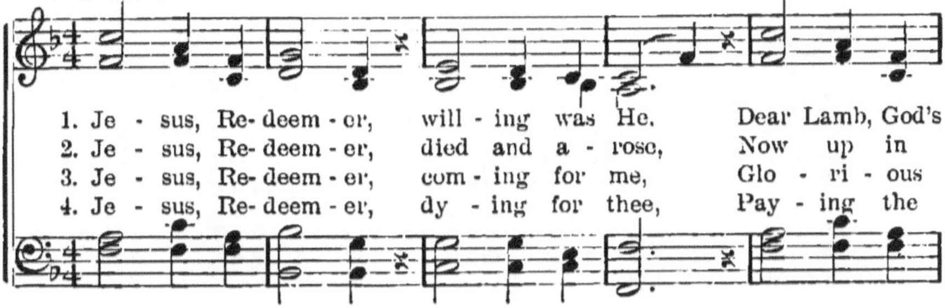

1. Je - sus, Re- deem - er, will - ing was He. Dear Lamb, God's
2. Je - sus, Re- deem - er, died and a - rose, Now up in
3. Je - sus, Re- deem - er, com - ing for me, Glo - ri - ous
4. Je - sus, Re- deem - er, dy - ing for thee, Pay - ing the

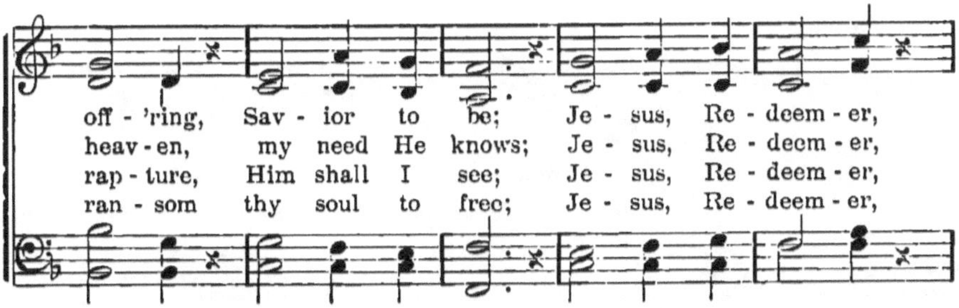

off - 'ring, Sav - ior to be; Je - sus, Re - deem - er,
heav - en, my need He knows; Je - sus, Re - deem - er,
rap - ture, Him shall I see; Je - sus, Re - deem - er,
ran - som thy soul to free; Je - sus, Re - deem - er,

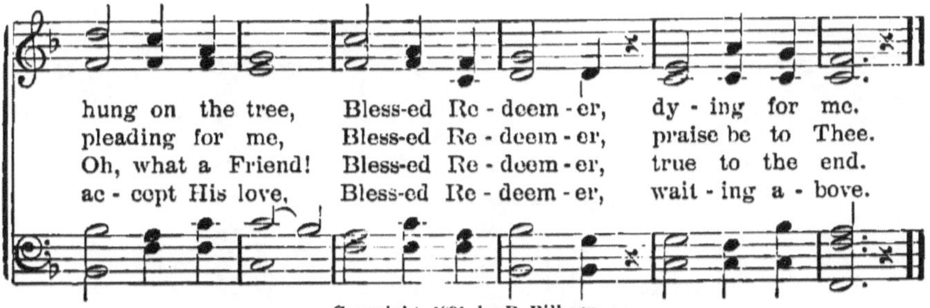

hung on the tree, Bless-ed Re - deem - er, dy - ing for me.
pleading for me, Bless-ed Re - deem - er, praise be to Thee.
Oh, what a Friend! Bless-ed Re - deem - er, true to the end.
ac - cept His love, Bless-ed Re - deem - er, wait - ing a - bove.

No. 116. Jesus is Waiting for Me.

C. H. G. CHAS. H. GABRIEL. By per.

1 Long sail-ing on life's trou-bled sea, In tem-pest, in storm and thro' calm,
2 From o - ver the wa-ters so dark, The cry of the Sav-ior I heard.
3 Now rest-ing so calmly in Him, My voy-age shall ev-er be sweet,

I yield-ed and anchored at last In Je-sus the cru-ci-fied Lamb.
He called me in ac-cents so sweet, I yield-ed, o - bey-ing His word.
With Him at the helm I am safe, What-ev-er the dan-ger I meet.

CHORUS.

Hal-le-lu - - jah, 'tis done,.... My soul.... now is free;....
Hal-le-lu-jah, 'tis done, 'tis done, My soul now is free, is free;

I am saved.... by His blood,.... And Je-sus is wait-ing for me.
I am saved by His blood, His blood,

No. 117. Redeemed.

FANNY J. CROSBY. W. J. KIRKPATRICK.

1. Redeemed, how I love to proclaim it, Redeemed by the blood of the Lamb;
2. Redeemed, and so hap-py in Je - sus, No language my rapture can tell,
3. I think of my bless-ed Re-deem - er, I think of Him all the day long,
4. I know I shall see in His beau - ty, The King in whose laws I delight,
5. I know there's a crown that is waiting In yonder bright mansion for me,

Redeemed thro' His in-fi-nite mer-cy, His child, and for-ev-er I am.
I know that the light of His pres-ence With me doth con-tin-ual-ly dwell.
I sing, for I can not be si - lent, His love is the theme of my song.
Who lov-ing-ly guard-eth my foot-steps, And giveth me songs in the night.
And soon with the spirits made perfect, At home with the Lord I shall be.

REFRAIN.

Re - deemed, re - deemed, Redeemed by the blood of the Lamb,
Redeemed, redeemed,

Re - deemed, re - deemed, His child, and for - ev - er I am.
Redeemed, redeemed,

By permission.

No. 118.   What a Savior.

Rev. G. W. Crofts.   P. Bilhorn.

1. What a won-der-ful Sav-ior is Je - sus, All our
2. Gen - tly in the green pas-tures He leads us, By the
3. Wide - ly o - pen the por-tals of glo - ry, To the
4. Oh, the hope that in full - ness He gives us! Oh, the

sins He hath borne on the tree; Of all guilt and transgressions He
wa - ters un - troubled and clear, With the man - na of heav-en He
cit - y whose streets are of gold, As He tells us the won - der - ful
joy and the peace, how di - vine! When in love He so free - ly re-

frees us, What a won - der - ful Sav - ior is He.
feeds us, And in sor - row He ev - er is near.
sto - ry, That to sin - ners so oft - en He told.
ceives us, And our souls in His right-eous - ness shine.

Chorus.

What a Sav - - ior, Sav - - ior,
What a won - der - ful Sav - ior, won - der - ful Sav - ior,

What a Savior. Concluded.

Won-der-ful Sav-ior is Je-sus, What a Sav - ior,
What a won-der-ful Sav-ior,

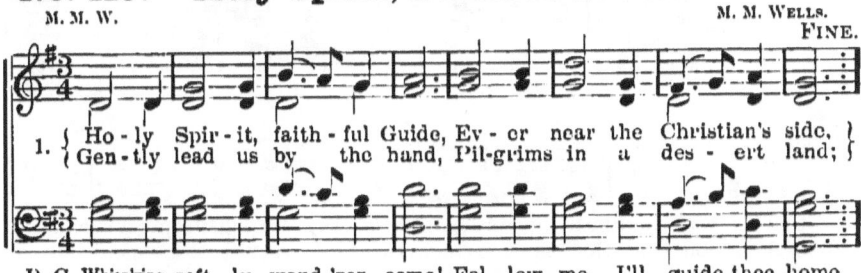

Sav - ior, What a won-der-ful Sav-ior is He.
Won-der-ful Sav-ior,

No. 119. Holy Spirit, Faithful Guide.

M. M. W.   M. M. WELLS.
FINE.

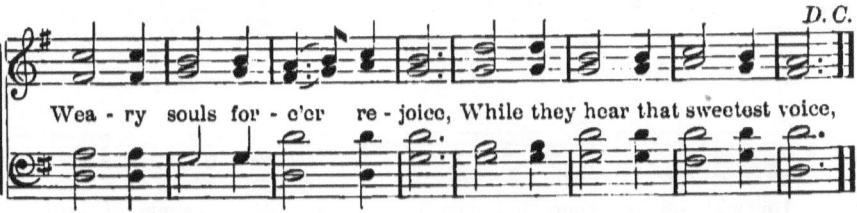

1. { Ho-ly Spir-it, faith-ful Guide, Ev-er near the Christian's side, }
   { Gen-tly lead us by the hand, Pil-grims in a des-ert land; }

D. C. Whisp'ring soft-ly, wand'rer, come! Fol-low me, I'll guide thee home.

D. C.

Wea-ry souls for-e'er re-joice, While they hear that sweetest voice,

2 Ever present, truest Friend,
Ever near, Thine aid to lend,
Leave us not to doubt and fear,
Groping on in darkness drear.
When the storms are raging sore,
Hearts grow faint, and hopes give o'er;
Whisper softly, wand'rer, come!
Follow me, I'll guide thee home.

3 When our days of toil shall cease,
Waiting still for sweet release,
Nothing left but heaven and prayer,
Wond'ring if our names are there;
Wading deep the dismal flood,
Pleading naught but Jesus' blood;
Whisper softly, wand'rer, come!
Follow me, I'll guide thee home.

No. 120. God is Coming.

Mrs. Sue M. O. Hoffman.

1. God is com-ing! God is com-ing! shout a-loud the glad re-frain:
2. God is com-ing! God is com-ing! roll the notes of joy on high;
3. God is com-ing! God is com-ing! and the hosts of sin are strong;
4. God is com-ing! God is com-ing! oh, lift up your heart and pray!

Send the cry from town and cit - y to the vil - lage, ham-let, plain;
Ev - 'ry blood-bought son of Je - sus, ral - ly to your lead-er's cry!
We will meet them brave-ly, bold - ly, and the fight will not be long.
In the fight 'twixt light and darkness He will need strong arms to-day.

D. S. *Ev - 'ry man be up on du - ty, For Je - ho - vah comes this way.*

God is com - ing! hear the an - gels shout the tid-ings from a - bove!
God is com - ing! God is com - ing! rub your rust - y ar - mor bright,
God is com - ing! and be - fore Him pow'rs of darkness must give way;
God is com - ing! fal - ter nev - er—when the con-flict here is done

He will del - uge your whole country with His ti - dal wave of love.
Gird your sword and shield a - bout you, and be read - y for the fight.
God is com - ing! by His strong arm we shall gain the vic - to - ry.
You shall wear a crown of glo - ry in the king-dom of His Son.

God is Coming. Concluded.

CHORUS.

ff **D. C.**

God is com-ing! pass the watch-word all a - long the line to - day!

No. 121.   He Feedeth His Flock.

FANNY J. CROSBY.   JNO. R. SWENEY.

1. Oh, sweet is the voice of my Shepherd, Who leadeth me day by day,
2. When far from my Shep-herd I wandered, A-lone on the mountain cold,
3. And tho' I may walk thro' the shad-ow, No e - vil can harm me there;
4. Oh, sweet is the voice of my Shepherd, No oth-er so kind as He:

:S: **FINE.**

Who cov-ers my life with His mer - cy, And lov - ing-ly guides my way.
He car-ried me home from the dark-ness To rest in His own dear fold.
His rod and His staff are my com-fort, He mak-eth my soul His care.
The won-der-ful, won - der - ful Shepherd, Who laid down His life for me!

D. S. *He feed-eth His flock by the lil - ies, In beau - ti - ful vales that grow.*

CHORUS.   **D. S.**

He feedeth His flock at the noontide, Where fountains are murmuring low, ...

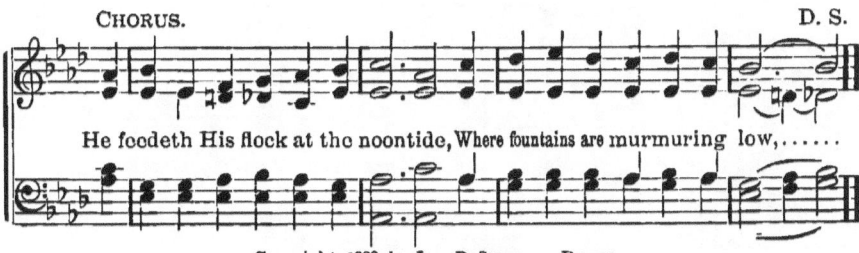

No. 122. Glorious Fountain.

COWPER.   T. C. O'KANE. By per.

1. There is a fountain filled with blood, filled with blood, filled with blood,
2. The dy-ing thief re-joiced to see, re-joiced to see, re-joiced to see,
3. Thou dying Lamb, Thy precious blood, Thy precious blood, Thy precious blood,
4. E'er since by faith I saw the stream, I saw the stream, I saw the stream,

There is a fount-ain filled with blood, Drawn from Immanuel's veins, And
The dy-ing thief re-joiced to see, That fountain in his day, And
Thou dy-ing Lamb, Thy precious blood Shall nev-er lose its power, Till
E'er since by faith I saw the stream, Thy flow-ing wounds sup-ply, Re-

sinners plunged beneath that flood, beneath that flood, beneath that flood, And
there may I, tho' vile as he, tho' vile as he, tho' vile as he, And
all the ransomed Church of God, Church of God, Church of God, Till
deeming love has been my theme, has been my theme, has been my theme. Re-

CHORUS.

sinners plunged beneath that flood, Lose all their guilty stains. ⎫
there may I, tho' vile as he, Wash all my sins a-way. ⎬ Oh, glo-ri-ous
all the ransomed Church of God Are saved to sin no more. ⎪
deeming love has been my theme And shall be till I die. ⎭

fountain! Here will I stay, And in Thee ev-er Wash my sins a-way.

No. 123. How can I but Love Him?

P. B.

P. BILHORN.

1. When I hear the grand old sto - ry, Of - ten told and
2. In the gar - den how He suf - fered, In the judg-ment
3. How to Cal - va - ry they led Him, As the cross He
4. To the cross they nailed my Sav - ior, With the nails His
5. Bleed - ing, suff' - ring, thirst - ing, dy - ing, Hear Him cry - ing

sung be - fore, How that Je - sus came from glo - ry,
hall He bore Cru - el mock-ings, scorn and spit - ting,
meek - ly bore, Crushed be - neath its heav - y bur - den,
flesh they tore, As I there be - hold Him pin - ioned,
o'er and o'er, God for - give them! God for - give them!

REFRAIN.

Then I love Him more and more; More and more,
'Twas for me; I'll love Him more; More and more,
Can I help but love Him more? More and more,
How can I but love Him more? More and more,
I will love Him more and more; More and more,

more and more, Then I love Him more and more.
more and more, 'Twas for me, I'll love Him more?
more and more, Can I help but love Him more?
more and more, How can I but love Him more?
more and more, I will love Him more and more.

Copyright, 1891, by P. Bilhorn.

No. 124. We'll Work till Jesus Comes.

Mrs. Elizabeth Mills.

Dr. Wm. Miller.
Arr. by W. J. K., 1859.

1. Oh, land of rest, for thee I sigh, When will the mo-ment come,
2. No tran-quil joys on earth I know, No peace-ful, shelt-'ring dome;
3. To Je-sus Christ I fled for rest; He bade me cease to roam,
4. I sought at once my Sav-ior's side, No more my steps shall roam;

When I shall lay my arm-or by, And dwell in peace at home?
This world's a wil-der-ness of woe, This world is not my home.
And lean for suc-cor on His breast Till He con-duct me home.
With Him I'll brave death's chill-ing tide, And reach my heav'n-ly home.

CHORUS.

We'll work till Je-sus comes, We'll work till Je-sus comes, We'll
We'll work We'll work

work till Je-sus comes, And we'll be gath-ered home.
We'll work

He Has Come.

Mrs. J. H. Knowles.

Mrs. Joseph F. Knapp.

1. He has come! He has come! My Re-deem-er has come, He has
2. He has come! He has come! My Love and my Lord, Ev-'ry
3. He has come to a-bide, And ho-ly must be The

tak-en my heart as His own chosen home; At last I have giv-en the
tho't of my be-ing is swayed by His word; He has come! and He rules in the
place where my Lord deigns to banquet with me; And this is my prayer, Lord,

wel-come He sought, He has come and His com-ing all glad-ness has bro't.
realm of my soul, And His scep-tre is love, O bless-ed con-trol!
since Thou art come, Make meet for Thy pres-ence my heart as Thy home.

CHORUS.

Joy! joy is mine, My Sav-ior di-vine, Comes to a-bide with me, with me;
with me,

Rit.

Come to a-bide, ev-er to a-bide, My own lov-ing Sav-ior a-bid-eth with me.

No. 126. Jesus Saves Me To-day.

P. B.

P. BILHORN.

1. Je-sus saves me to-day, and He saves me al-way, While I
2. I will sing of the Lord, for He saves me to-day, And He
3. I will come with thanks-giv-ing and make a glad noise, Un-to
4. 'Tis a won-der-ful tho't that the Sav-ior has brought Full sal-

trust in Je-ho-vah, my Lord; Nev-er need I to fear, for He
leads me in pas-tures so green; By the wa-ters so still, do-ing
Him be the praise ev-er-more; Je-sus saves me to-day, and He'll
va-tion for all who be-lieve; He will save you to-day, and He'll

ev-er is near, And He saves me to-day by His word.
God's ho-ly will, While His blood that was shed keeps me clean.
keep me al-way, Would to God I had known it be-fore.
keep you al-way, If you on-ly His word will re-ceive.

CHORUS.

Je-sus saves me to-day, hal-le-lu-jah! Je-sus

saves, and He keeps me al-way, Bless His name for His love,

Jesus Saves Me To-day. Concluded.

That He came from a-bove, Je-sus saves and He keeps me to-day.

No. 127. Heaven is not Far Away.

C. E. L.

C. E. Leslie. By per.

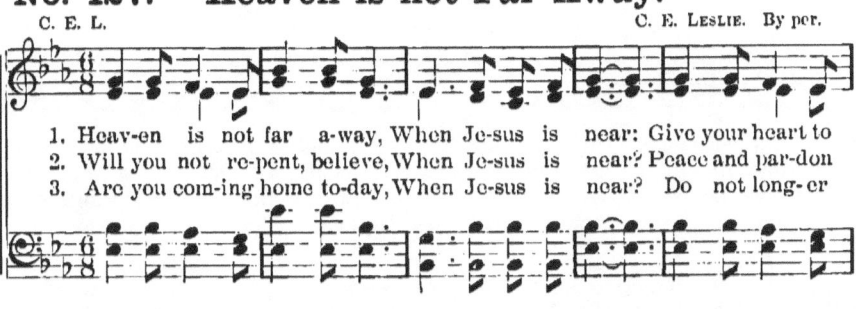

1. Heav-en is not far a-way, When Je-sus is near: Give your heart to
2. Will you not re-pent, believe, When Je-sus is near? Peace and par-don
3. Are you com-ing home to-day, When Je-sus is near? Do not long-er

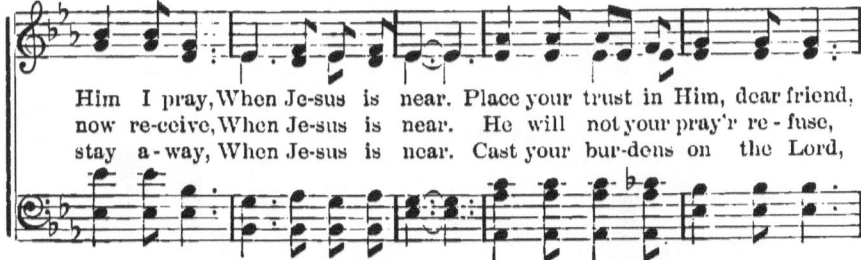

Him I pray, When Je-sus is near. Place your trust in Him, dear friend,
now re-ceive, When Je-sus is near. He will not your pray'r re-fuse,
stay a-way, When Je-sus is near. Cast your bur-dens on the Lord,

Rit.

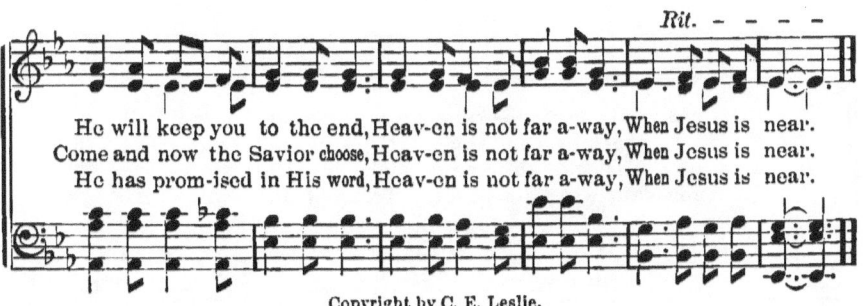

He will keep you to the end, Heav-en is not far a-way, When Jesus is near.
Come and now the Savior choose, Heav-en is not far a-way, When Jesus is near.
He has prom-ised in His word, Heav-en is not far a-way, When Jesus is near.

No. 128.   Oh, Could I Speak.

MEDLEY.   Arr. by MASON.

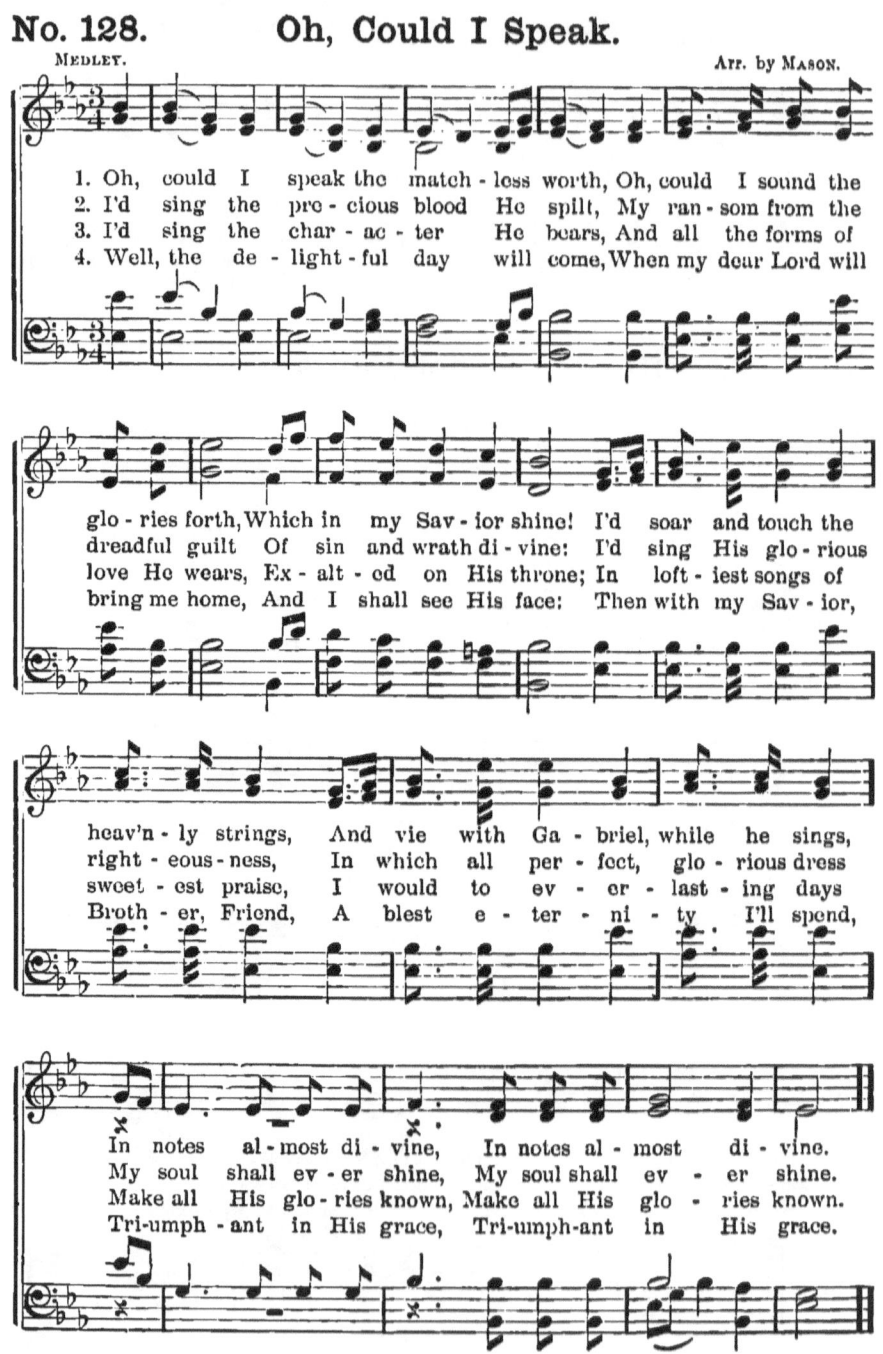

1. Oh, could I speak the match-less worth, Oh, could I sound the glo-ries forth, Which in my Sav-ior shine! I'd soar and touch the heav'n-ly strings, And vie with Ga-briel, while he sings, In notes al-most di-vine, In notes al-most di-vine.

2. I'd sing the pre-cious blood He spilt, My ran-som from the dreadful guilt Of sin and wrath di-vine: I'd sing His glo-rious right-eous-ness, In which all per-fect, glo-rious dress My soul shall ev-er shine, My soul shall ev-er shine.

3. I'd sing the char-ac-ter He bears, And all the forms of love He wears, Ex-alt-ed on His throne; In loft-iest songs of sweet-est praise, I would to ev-er-last-ing days Make all His glo-ries known, Make all His glo-ries known.

4. Well, the de-light-ful day will come, When my dear Lord will bring me home, And I shall see His face: Then with my Sav-ior, Broth-er, Friend, A blest e-ter-ni-ty I'll spend, Tri-umph-ant in His grace, Tri-umph-ant in His grace.

No. 129. My Spirit is Free.

W. A. S.

Rev. W. A. Spencer. By per.

1. I fol-low the foot-steps of Je-sus, my Lord, His
2. A lep-er He found me, pol-lut-ed by sin, From
3. A cap-tive in woe to my pris-on of night The
4. Pro-claim it, 'tis done, full sal-va-tion is wrought For

Spir-it doth lead me a-long; I walk in the path-way made
which He a-lone can set free; He spake in His mer-cy, "I
Mas-ter hath o-pen'd the door; Shout a-loud of de-liv-'rance, ye
sin-ners from sor-row and woe; Sing a-loud of His grace who my

plain by His word, And He fills all my soul with this song.
will, be thou clean," And He in-stant-ly pu-ri-fied me.
an-gels of light, Praise His name, oh, my soul, ev-er-more.
par-don has bought; "For His blood wash-es whit-er than snow."

CHORUS.

Glo-ry to God! my spir-it is free, Glo-ry to God, He pu-ri-fies me! I'm

walking the thorn-path, but joyful I'll be While fol-low-ing Je-sus, my Lord.

No. 130. Happy in the Love of Jesus.

HENRIETTA E. BLAIR.　　　　　　　　　　　WM. J. KIRKPATRICK. By per.

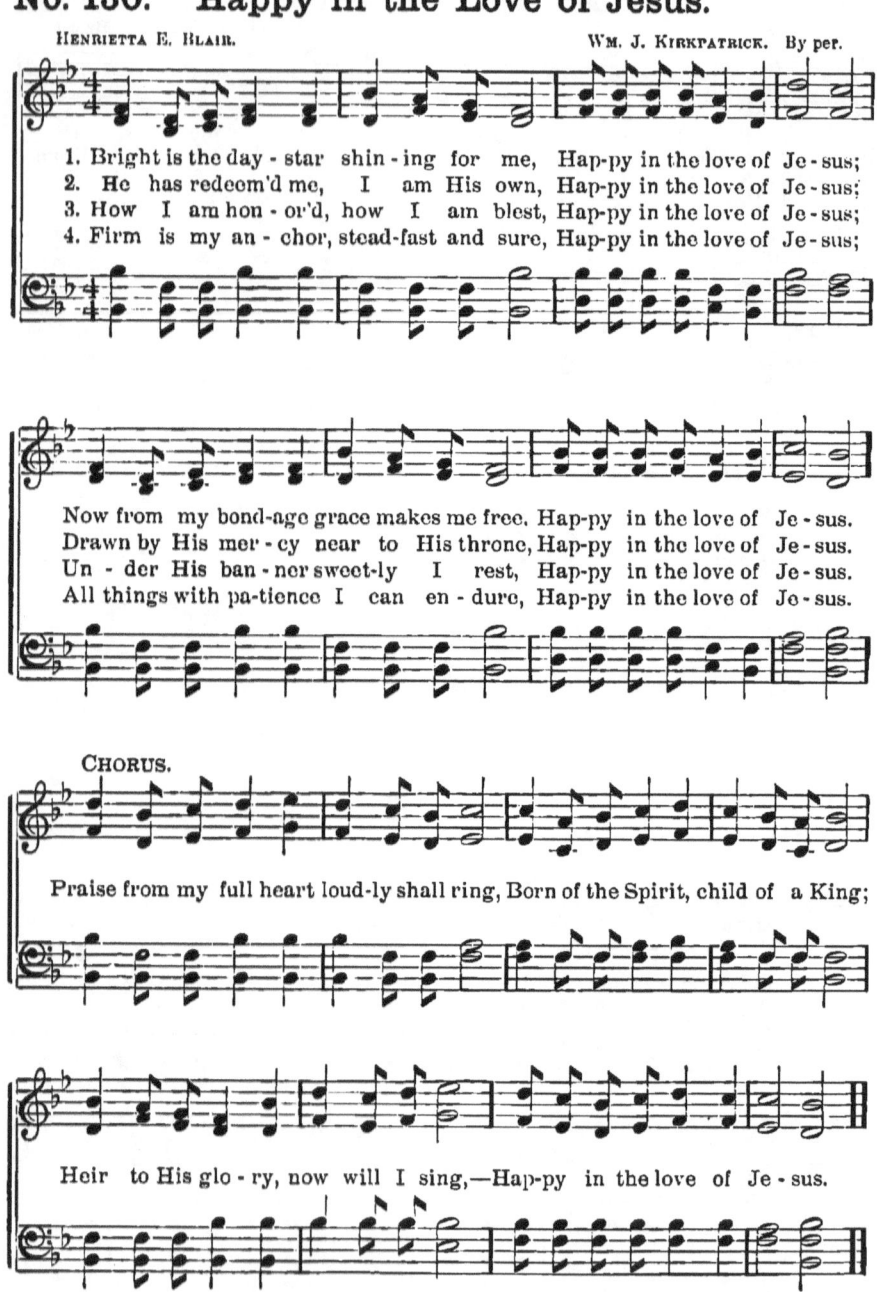

1. Bright is the day-star shin-ing for me, Hap-py in the love of Je-sus;
2. He has redeem'd me, I am His own, Hap-py in the love of Je-sus;
3. How I am hon-or'd, how I am blest, Hap-py in the love of Je-sus;
4. Firm is my an-chor, stead-fast and sure, Hap-py in the love of Je-sus;

Now from my bond-age grace makes me free, Hap-py in the love of Je-sus.
Drawn by His mer-cy near to His throne, Hap-py in the love of Je-sus.
Un-der His ban-ner sweet-ly I rest, Hap-py in the love of Je-sus.
All things with pa-tience I can en-dure, Hap-py in the love of Je-sus.

CHORUS.

Praise from my full heart loud-ly shall ring, Born of the Spirit, child of a King;

Heir to His glo-ry, now will I sing,—Hap-py in the love of Je-sus.

Only Believe.

O. S. GRINNELL. By per.

1. Je - sus Christ is now a - mong us, On - ly be - lieve!
2. Is there one that's seek - ing par - don, On - ly be - lieve!
3. Je - sus comes to sanc - ti - fy you, On - ly be - lieve!

He is here to bless and save us, On - ly be - lieve!
Cast on Him your heav - y bur - den, On - ly be - lieve!
And His blood will pu - ri - fy you, On - ly be - lieve!

He is lov - ing, kind, and gracious, And His blood is ef - fi - ca - cious;
Let not sa - tan long - er grieve you, Nor the world and sin de - ceive you;
Glo - ry, hon - or, praise and pow - er, Be un - to the Lamb for - ev - er;

Ev - 'ry soul may feel Him pre - cious, On - ly be - lieve!
Christ, the Lord, will now re - ceive you, On - ly be - lieve!
From all sin He doth de - liv - er, On - ly be - lieve!

No. 132. Having done All, to Stand.

Miss J. H. Johnston.   P. Bilhorn.

1. Sol-dier of Christ, be stead-fast! This is the "e - vil day;"
2. Pa-tient and true and faith-ful, Fac - ing the dead - ly foe;
3. This is no time to ques - tion, This is no time to yield;

Look to your Roy - al Lead - er, Ev - er His word o - bey.
Stand in the place ap - point - ed, March, when He bids 'you go.
Nev - er a soul should fal - ter, Bear - ing His sword and shield.

Tak - ing the heav'n-ly ar - mor, Wait for your Lord's com - mand;
All through the pass - ing mo-ments, On - ward to Ca - naan's land;
Keep in the ranks of Je - sus, Watch-ing on ev - 'ry hand;

This is the charge He gives you, "Hav - ing done all, to stand."
Ban - ish all fear and doubt-ing, Hav - ing done all, to stand.
This is the chris-tian du - ty, "Hav - ing done all, to stand."

CHORUS.

Stand, there - fore, stand, Stand, there - fore, stand; Trust - ing in

Having done All, to Stand. Concluded.

Je - sus, our Sav - ior, Hav - ing done all to stand.

No. 133. My Title's Clear.

P. BILHORN.

1. Since I can read my ti - tle clear, To man - sions in the skies,
2. Should earth a - gainst my soul en - gage, And fier - y darts be hurled,
3. Let cares like a wild del - uge come, Let storms of sor - row fall—
4. There I shall bathe my wea - ry soul In seas of heav'n - ly rest,

I'll bid fare - well to ev - 'ry fear, And wipe my weep - ing eyes.
Then I can smile at Sa - tan's rage, And face a frown - ing world.
So I but safe - ly reach my home, My God, my heav'n, my all.
And not a wave of troub - le roll A - cross my peace - ful breast.

I'll stand, (I'll stand,) the storm, (the storm,) I've an - chored in the vail;

ff

Tho' Sa - tan fier - y darts may hurl, Thro' Christ I shall pre - vail.

In the Morning.

LIZZIE EDWARDS.

JNO. R. SWENEY. By per.

1. We are pil - grims look - ing home, Sad and wea - ry, oft we
2. Oh, these ten - der bro - ken ties, How they dim our ach - ing
3. When our fet - tered souls are free, Far be - yond the nar - row
4. Thro' our pil - grim jour - ney here, Tho' the night is sometimes

roam, But we know 'twill all be well in the morn - ing;
eyes, But like jew - els they will shine in the morn - ing;
sea, And we hear the Sav - ior's voice in the morn - ing;
drear, Let us watch and per - se - vere till the morn - ing;

When, our an - chor safe - ly cast, Ev - 'ry storm - y wave is
When our vic - tor palms we bear, And our robes im - mor - tal
When our gold - en sheaves we bring To the feet of Christ our
Then our high - est trib - ute raise For the love that crowns our

D. S. sun - ny re - gion

FINE.

past, And we gath - er safe at last in the morn - ing.
wear, We shall know each oth - er there in the morn - ing.
King, What a cho - rus we shall sing in the morn - ing.
days, And to Je - sus give the praise in the morn - ing.

bright, When we hail the bless - ed light in the morn - ing.

Copyright, 1884, by John J. Hood.

In the Morning. Concluded.

CHORUS.

When we all meet a-gain in the morn - ing, On the sweet, blooming

D. S.

hills in the morn - ing; Nev-er more to say good night In that

No. 135. Happy Land.

Old Melody.

1. There is a hap-py land, Far, far a - way, Where saints in glo-ry stand,
2. Bright, in that hap-py land, Beams ev-'ry eye: Kept by a Father's hand,
3. Come to that hap-py land, Come, come a - way; Why will you doubting stand?

Bright, bright as day; Oh, how they sweet-ly sing, "Wor-thy is our
Love can - not die. On, then, to glo - ry run; Be a crown and
Why still de - lay? Oh, we shall hap - py be When from sin and

Sav - ior King," Loud let His prais - es ring, Praise, praise for aye!
king-dom won; And bright, a - bove the sun. Reign ev - er-more.
sor - row free; Lord, we shall dwell with Thee, Blest ev - er-more.

No. 136.　We'll Be There.

I. B.

I. BALTZELL.

1. I love to think of my heav'nly home, Where all shall glo-ry share,
2. I love to think of my heav'nly home, So free from toil and care;
3. I love to think of my heav'nly home, Where saints shall white robes wear,
4. I love to think of my heav'nly home, So love-ly and so rare;

Where songs of rap-ture shall ev - er rise: Oh, tell me, will you all be there?
Where crowns of vic - t'ry shall nev - er fade: Oh, tell me, will you all be there?
And sing sweet an-thems for ev - er-more: Oh, tell me, will you all be there?
A few more years and I'll reach the goal: Oh, tell me, will you all be there?

CHORUS. Arr.

We'll be there,　We'll be there,　At the sound-ing of the
Hal- le- lu-jah,　Hal- le-lu-jah,

trum-pet, we'll be there.　We'll be there,　We'll be
We'll be there,　Hal - le - lu - jah,

there,　At the sounding of the trumpet, we'll be there.
Hal - le -lu- jah,　　　　　　　　　　　　we'll be there.

No. 137. Why Not Receive Him?

ADA BLENKHORN.

P. BILHORN.

1. The Prince of glo - ry left His throne, The sin-ner's friend to be;
2. He feeds the hun-gry soul with bread From life's e - ter - nal tree,
3. He dwells be - fore the great white throne, For need - y souls to pray:

His ho - ly brow with thorns was crowned, He died on Cal - va - ry:
And bids the thirst - y spir - it drink From liv - ing foun-tains, free:
He pleads for those to come to Him, Who did their Lord be - tray:

CHORUS.

He suf-fered thus for thee.)
He of - fers this to thee. } Why not re-ceive Him? Why not be-lieve Him?
He call - eth thee to - day.)

While He is call - ing, Call-ing to - day; I will re-ceive Him,

I will be-lieve Him; While He is call - ing, I'll trust in Him to - day.

No. 138. He is Just the Same To-day.

Mrs. S. Z. KAUFMAN. Heb. 13: 8. I. N. McHose.

1. Have you ev - er heard the sto - ry of the Babe of Beth-le-
2. Have you ev - er heard how Je - sus walk'd up - on the roll - ing
3. Once while rest - ing on a pil - low in the ves - sel fast a-
4. Sure - ly you have heard how Je - sus prayed down in Geth-sem - a-

hem, Who was wor-shiped by the an - gels and by wise and ho - ly
sea, To His dear dis - ci - ples toss - ing on the waves of Gal - i-
sleep, There a - rose a might - y tem-pest on the wild and rag - ing
ne, How He shed His pre-cious life-blood on the rug-ged, shame-ful

men, How He taught the learn-ed doc - tors in the Tem - ple far a-
lee, How He res - cued sink-ing Pe - ter from his dan - ger and dis-
deep; "Peace, be still," the Lord command-ed, ev - 'ry an - gry wave did
tree, Cru - el thorns His fore-head pierc-ing as His spir - it passed a-

way? I am glad to tell you, sin - ners, He is just the same to - day.
may? I am glad to tell you, sin - ners, He is just the same to - day.
stay: I am glad to tell you, sin - ners, He is just the same to - day.
way; Sin-ner, won't you come and love Him? He is just the same to - day.

He is Just the Same To-day. Concluded.

CHORUS.

He's just the same to-day, Yes, just the same to-day, I'm

glad to tell you, sin-ner, He is just the same to-day.

No. 139. Death and Eternity.

C. H. G.

CHAS. H. GABRIEL.

Feelingly.

1. Coming when the day is bright, Com-ing in the si-lent night,
2. Coming to the gay and proud, Com-ing with a snow-white shroud,
3. Coming with un-hin-dered sway, Com-ing ev-'ry fleet-ing day,
4. Coming to the sin-ful one, Com-ing when our life is done,

p Slow ad lib.   Echo.

Coming at the morning light,
Coming to the gray head bowed,   } Coming, coming, death and e-ter-ni-ty, e-ter-ni-ty.
Coming to the young and gay,
Gath'ring to the judgment throne,

No. 140. They Sing a New Song.

JULIA H. JOHNSTON. P. BILHORN.

1. High in yon-der heavenly courts the ransomed sing, Cast-ing down their
2. Oh, the wondrous song of Love, at last com-plete! Oh, the gold-en
3. On-ly those whose robes are washed, can join that throng, None but lips at-

gold-en crowns be-fore their King, Ban-ished ev-cry grief and fear and
vi - als, full of o - dors sweet; Thro' the ris - en Sav-ior, once for
tuned by grace can sing that song; Cleanse us, bless-ed Sav - ior from the

earth - ly wrong, While the saints redeemed now join the glad new song.
sin - ners slain, We as kings and priests to God shall ev - er reign.
stain of sin, Let the glo-rious song of heav-en now be - gin!

CHORUS.

Sing . . . ing to the Lamb . . . . who once was
Sing-ing to the Lamb, Sing-ing to the Lamb,

slain on Cal - va - ry; Sing . . . ing to the
slain on Cal - va - ry, Cal-va- ry; Sing-ing to the Lamb,

Copyright, 1891, by P. Bilhorn.

They Sing a New Song. Concluded.

Lamb................ Who ev - er lives e - ter - nal - ly.
Sing - ing to the Lamb lives e - ter - nal - ly.

No. 141. In Time of Need.

JULIA H. JOHNSTON.   A. BEIRLY. By per

1. Fear not the path-less wil - der-ness, O heav'n-ward pil-grim, on-ward press;
2. The tempter's darts may oft as - sail, But hope and cour- age nev - er fail;
3. In storm and dark-ness and dis- may, A hand di - vine shall guide the way;

FINE.

His word of prom - ise bold - ly plead, Who giv - eth help in time of need.
Lift up thy heart, dis-miss thy fear, For One who loves thy soul is near.
Till Canaan's shore is won at last, And all thy "time of need" is past.
D.S. *Come near-er still, it is His will To give thee help in time of need.*

REFRAIN.   D. S.

In time of need, in time of need, His prom-ise true, sin-cere- ly plead;

No. 142.   Christ is All.

W. A. Williams.

1. I en-tered once a home of care, For age and pen-u-ry were there,
2. I stood be-side a dy-ing bed, Where lay a child with aching head,
3. I saw the mar-tyr at the stake, The flames could not his courage shake,
4. Then come to Christ, oh, come to-day, The Fa-ther, Son, and Spir-it say:

Yet peace and joy with-al; I asked the lone-ly moth-er whence
Wait-ing for Je-sus' call; I marked his smile, 'twas sweet as May,
Nor death His soul ap-pall, I asked him whence his strength was giv'n,
The Bride re-peats the call, For He will cleanse your guilt-y stains,

Her help-less wid-ow-hood's de-fense, She told me "Christ was all."
And as his spir-it passed a-way, He whispered, "Christ is all."
He looked tri-umphant-ly to heaven, And answered, "Christ is all."
His love will soothe your weary pains, For "Christ is all in all."

CHORUS.

Christ is all, all in all, Yes, Christ is all in all;

Christ is all, all in all. Yes, Christ is all in all.

By permission of S. T. Gordon.

No. 143.   Come, Ye Weary.

C. E.

P. BILHORN.

1. Come, ye wea - ry, heav - y la - den, Burden'd with your sins and fears;
2. Cast on Him your heav - y bur - den, He has prom-ised to sus - tain;
3. He was tempt - ed like as we are, And He knows our fee - ble frame;
4. He will help you sin to con - quer, Give you vic - t'ry in the fight;

There is One who will re - ceive you, When He sees re - pent - ant tears.
None have ev - er asked His guid - ance Who have ev - er asked in vain.
Faith - ful - ly He keeps His prom - ise He is ev - er - more the same.
He is will - ing to trans - late you, Out of dark - ness in - to light.

CHORUS.

Come, ye wea - ry, heav - y la - den, Je - sus waits to give you rest; . .

Come, and He will give you wel - come, To the man - sions of the blest.

No. 144.   He Saved Me, Hallelujah!

E. A. H.   Rev. Elisha A. Hoffman.

1. I earn-est-ly pray'd for de-liv-'rance from sin, And longed to be
2. My feet had been tread-ing the path-way of sin; My robes were de-
3. And now I'm re-joic-ing in Je-sus my King, And songs of thanks-

washed from de-file-ment with-in; To Je-sus for par-don and
filed and my spir-it un-clean; I went to the Sav-ior, the
giv-ing un-ceas-ing-ly sing; I praise and a-dore Him, the

cleans-ing I came, And He saved me, hal-le-lu-jah to His
dear Son of God, And He washed me and He cleansed me in His
dear Lamb of God, Who washed me and re-deemed me in His

CHORUS.

won-der-ful name!)
won-der-ful blood! } He washed me, hal-le-lu-jah! He cleansed me, hal-le-
won-der-ful blood!)

lu-jah! He saved me, hal-le-lu-jah to His won-der-ful name!

No. 145. Oh, be Ready.

ADA BLENKHORN. P. BILHORN.

1. The judg-ment day is com-ing, Oh, be read-y when the
2. Ye who re-ject sal-va-tion, Oh, be read-y when the
3. Be-hold, the Bridegroom com-eth, Oh, be read-y when the
4. Why long-er grieve the spir-it, Oh, be read-y when the

trum-pet calls, To stand be-fore the Mas-ter, Oh, be
trum-pet calls, For you was Je-sus smit-ten, Oh, be
trum-pet calls, Will you not haste to meet Him? Oh, be
trum-pet calls; Come make your peace with Je-sus, Oh, be

CHORUS.

read-y when the trum-pet calls. Oh, be read-y! Oh, be read-y!

Oh, be read-y when the Mas-ter calls; Oh, be read-y!

Oh, be read-y! Oh, be read-y when the Mas-ter calls!

No. 146.   Redemption.

F. J. CROSBY.   PETER BILHORN.

1. O won - der - ful words of the Gos - pel! O won - der - ful
2. He came from the throne of His glo - ry, And left the bright
3. O come to this won - der - ful Sav - ior, Come wea - ry and
4. There's no oth - er re - uge but Je - sus, No shel - ter where

mes-sage they bring, Pro - claim - ing a bless-ed re-demp-tion Thro'
mansions a - bove, The world to re-deem from its bond-age; So
sor - row-op - pressed; Be - hold on the cross how He suf-fered, That
lost ones may fly; And now, while He's ten-der-ly call - ing: O

CHORUS.

Je - sus our Sav - ior and King.
great His com-pas - sion and love.
you in His king-dom might rest.
"turn ye," "for why will ye die?"

Be - lieve, oh, be-lieve in His

mer-cy That flows like a foun - tain so free; Be - lieve, and re-

Redemption. Concluded.

Rit. - - -

ceive the re-demp-tion He of - fers to you and to me.

Fully Persuaded.

Rev. E. A. HOFFMAN. J. H. TENNEY. By per.

1. God in His mer - cy calls up - on me, I'm ful - ly per-
2. Je - sus en - treats me so ten - der - ly, I'm ful - ly per-
3. Heav-en now of - fers par - don to me, I'm ful - ly per-

REFRAIN.

suad - ed A Christian to be.
suad - ed A Christian to be. I'm ful - ly per - suad - ed,
suad - ed A Christian to be.

Ful - ly per-suad-ed, Ful - ly per-suad-ed A Christian to be.

Copyright, 1878, by J. H. Tenney.

No. 148. I Long to Work for Thee.

Rev. WILLIAM FAWCETT.

W. S. NICKLE.

1. Je - sus, and may I work for Thee, A mor - tal man from
2. To work for Thee, the Morn - ing Star, That saw me lost, and
3. To work for Thee, my dear - est Friend, On whom my ev - 'ry

sin set free? A mor - tal man with short'ning days, Per-
from a - far Shed o'er my soul a light di - vine, And
hope de - pends; Who washed a - way my earth - ly shame, And

CHORUS.

mit - ted thus to work and praise.)
com - fort - ed this heart of mine. } I'll work for Thee, I'll
gave to me a new, best name.)

work for Thee, Yes, dear - est Lord, I'll work for Thee.

4 Yes, blessed Jesus, yes, I may
Go work for Thee throughout this day,
And all the joy or good I crave,
Is but some fallen soul to save.

5 I'll work for Thee, Thou blessed One,
Eternal God, eternal Son,
And boast, but never boast in vain,
I'll work for Him who once was slain.

No. 149. Standing! Knocking! Pleading!

Arr. by P. B.

P. BILHORN.

1. The Sav - ior now is stand - ing Out - side the fast closed door;
2. The Sav - ior now is knock - ing: And lo! His hand is scarred,
3. The Sav - ior now is plead - ing In ac - cents meek and low·

In lone - ly pa - tience wait - ing, To pass the thres - hold o'er;
And thorns his brow en - cir - cles, And tears his face have marred;
He died for you my broth - er Oh! why then treat him so?

He waits to bring you com - fort, Your bur - dens sore to bear,
Oh love that pass - eth knowl - edge So pa - tient - ly to wait!
Bow down with shame and sor - row, Swing o - pen wide the door

Oh! why then will you lin - ger And keep Him stand - ing there.
Oh! heart so vile and sin - ful, So fast to bar the gate.
And bid Him, en - ter, en - ter, To leave you nev - er more.

No. 150.   Hold up Your Hand for Jesus.

(A little street boy in London had both legs broken by a dray passing over them. He was laid in one of the beds of the hospital to die, and another little fellow was laid near by, picked up sick with famine and fever. The latter was allowed to lie down by the side of the little crushed boy. He crept up to him and said: ' Bubby, did you never hear about Jesus?" "No, I never heard of Him " "Bubby, I went to the Mission School once, and they told us that Jesus would take you to heaven when you die, and you'd never have hunger any more—and no more pain—if you axed Him." " I couldn't ask such a great big gentleman as He to do anything for me. He wouldn't stop to speak to a little boy like me." " But He'll do all that if you ax Him." " How can I ax Him if I don't know where He lives, and how can I get there when both my legs is broke?" " Bubby, they told me at Mission School as how Jesus passes by. Teacher says as how He goes around. How do you know but that He might come around to the hospital this very night? You'd know Him if you was to see Him " "But I can't keep my eyes open. My legs feel so awful bad. Doctor says I'll die." ' Bubby, hold up your hand, and He'll know what you want when He passes by." They got the hand up. It dropped. Tried again. It slowly fell back. Three times he got up the little hand, only to let it fall. Bursting into tears, he said: "I give it up." " Bubby, lend me yer hand, put yer elbow on my pillow, I can do without it " Soon the hand was propped up. And when they came in the morning the boy lay dead, his hand still held up for Jesus.)

Theo D. C. Miller, M. D.   Warren W. Bentley.

SOLO.

1. A lit-tle child lay dy-ing, With none to soothe his pain;
2. "I want to speak of Je-sus, Be-fore my eyes grow dim;"
3. "I could not ask a stran-ger This dy-ing form to see;
4. "Oh, now I'm sure-ly dy-ing, My eyes are grow ing dim;
5. The lit-tle hand so fee-ble Went up, but fell a-gain;

INST.

No moth-er's face to cheer him, And give him smiles a-gain;
The poor boy gen-tly whis-pered, "I nev-er heard of Him."
And one so good and no-ble Would nev-er speak to me,
In pain I can-not lin-ger— How shall I speak to Him?"
Then twice he slow-ly raised it, But could not bear the pain;

But one brave lit-tle fel-low Crept slow ly to his bed,
"But He is ev-er near you; And when this life is o'er,
I know not where to find Him, If He would ease my pain;
"Hold up your hand for Je-sus, And when He pass-es by,
Then propp'd up on a pil-low, With sad eyes o-pened wide.

By permission.

Hold up Your Hand. Concluded.

And, gaz-ing on his com-rade, In sooth-ing ac-cents said,
He'll take you up to heav-en, Where pain can come no more."
But tell me more of Je-sus, Oh! speak of Him a-gain!"
He'll take you in His bo-som, And bear you to the sky."
His hand went up for Je-sus, And bright with smiles he died.

CHORUS.

"I want to tell you, Wil-lie, Of One who lives on high;

Hold up your hand for Je-sus, This night He pass-es by;

Hold up your hand for Je-sus, This night He pass-es by."

No. 151. He Calleth for Thee.

ADA BLENKHORN. PETER BILHORN.

1. He is call-ing thee, my broth-er, He is call-ing thee to-day,
2. Now a-rise and say,"My Fa-ther, I have sinn'd and griev'd Thee sore,
3. Ere thou reach-est home He'll see thee and will hast-en thee to greet,
4. He will spread for thee a ban-quet, all the saved will join the throng,

Why from Him in cold and hun-ger wilt thou roam? He so
I have spurned Thy lov-ing fa-vor man-y years; Oh, have
With His arms out-stretched to clasp thee to His breast; He will
He will clothe thee in a robe of right-eous-ness; All the

pa-tient-ly en-treat-eth thee no long-er to de-lay,
mer-cy, I be-seech Thee, Thy for-give-ness I im-plore;
glad-ly give thee wel-come and with ten-der-ness will meet;
saints and an-gels gath-er round the throne will sing the song

For there's food and shel-ter wait-ing thee at home.
With a par-don ban-ish all my doubts and fears.
Thou at home wilt be thy Fa-ther's fa-vored guest.
Of re-demp-tion— and the Fa-ther's name will bless.

He Calleth for Thee. Concluded.

CHORUS.

He is call - - - ing, He is call - - - ing,
He is call - ing thee, my broth-er, He is call - ing thee to - day,

He is call - ing thee, my broth-er, to come home, (to come home,)

He is call - - - ing, He is call - - - ing,
He is call - ing thee, my broth-er, He is call - ing thee to - day,

He is call - ing thee, my broth-er, to come home. (to come home.)

No. 152.   We Shall Know.

ANNIE HERBERT.   J. H. ANDERSON.

1. When the mists have rolled in splendor From the beau-ty of the hills,
2. If we err, in hu-man blindness, And for-get that we are dust;
3. We shall come with songs of glad-ness, We shall gath-er 'round His throne;

And the sun-shine falls in glad-ness, On the riv-ers and the rills,
If we miss the law of kind-ness When we strug-gle to be just,
Face to face with those that love us, We shall know as we are known;

We may read love's shin-ing let-ter In the rain-bow of the spray,
Snow-y wings of peace shall cov-er All the plain that hides a-way,
And the song of our re-demp-tion Shall re-sound thro' end-less day,

We shall know each oth-er bet-ter When the mists have cleared a-way.
When the wea-ry watch is o-ver, And the mists have cleared a-way.
Prais-ing Him whose love has kept us Till the mists have cleared a-way.

We Shall Know. Concluded.

CHORUS.

We shall know........ as we are known,.......... Nev-er
We shall know   as we are known,

more.......... to walk a-lone,   In the
Nev-er more   to walk a-lone,

dawn - - - ing of the morning, When the mists....... have cleared a-
In the dawning of the morning,   When the mists

way;   In the dawn - - - ing of the morn-ing,
have cleared a-way   In the dawn-ing

When the mists........... have cleared a - way.
When the mists   have cleared a-way.

No. 153. The Sinner and the Song.

W. L. T.

WILL. L. THOMPSON.

SOLO.

ORGAN.

1 A sin-ner was wand'ring at e - ven-tide, His tempt-er was
2. He stopped and list-en'd to ev-'ry sweet chord, He re-membered the

watch-ing close by at his side, In his heart raged a bat - tle for
time he once loved the Lord, Come on! says the tempt-er, come

right a-gainst wrong, But hark! from the church he hears the sweet song.
on with the throng, But hark! from the church a - gain swells the song.

pp QUARTET.

1. Je - sus, lov - er of my soul, Let me to Thy bo - som fly,
2. While the bil-lows near me roll, While the tem-pest still is high.

SOLO.

ORGAN.

O tempt-er, de - part, I have served thee too long, I fly to the

By permission of Will. Thompson & Co.

The Sinner and the Song. Concluded.

Sav - ior, He dwells in that song, O Lord, can it be that a

sin - ner like me, May find a sweet ref - uge by com - ing to Thee?

pp QUARTET.

Oth - er ref - uge have I none, Hangs my helpless soul on Thee.

SOLO.

ORGAN.

I come, Lord, I come, Thou'lt for - give the dark past, And

pp QUARTET.

Oh, re - ceive my soul at last......

No. 154. Drifting Away From God.

Mrs. J. A. Griffith.

P. Bilhorn.

1. Drift-ing a-way from Christ in thy youth, Drift-ing a-way from
2. Drift-ing a-way from moth-er and home, Drift-ing a-way in
3. Drift-ing a-way on sin's treach'rous tide, Drift-ing where death and
4. Drift-ing a-way from hope's bless-ed shore, Drift-ing a-way where
5. Why will you drift on bil-lows of shame, Spurn-ing His grace a-

mer-cy and truth, Drift-ing to sin in ten-der-est youth,
sor-row to roam, Drift-ing where peace and rest can not come,
dark-ness a-bide, Drift-ing from heav'n a-way in your pride,
wild break-ers roar; Drift-ed and strand-ed, wreck'd, ev-er-more,
gain and a-gain? Soon you'll be lost! in sin to re-main,

CHORUS.

Drift-ing a-way from God.
Drift-ing a-way from God.
Drift-ing a-way from God.
Far from the light of God.
Ev-er a-way from God.

Broth-er, the Sav-ior has

called you be-fore; See! you are near-ing e-ter-ni-ty's shore!

Soon you may per-ish, be lost ev-er-more, Je-sus now calls for you.

No. 155. Welcome Home!

P. PALMER.

Mrs. J. F. KNAPP.

1. { Oh, when shall I sweep thro' the gates, The scenes of mor-tal - i - ty o'er?
   { What, then, for my spir- it a-waits? Will they on the glo - ri - ous shore?—

2. { Yes! lov'd ones who knew me be-fore, Who learn'd the new songs with me here,
   { In cho - rus will hail me, I know, And wel-come me home with good cheer!

CHORUS.

Wel - come home!   wel - come home!   A
Wel - come home!   wel - come home!

wel - come in glo - ry for me!   Wel - come
Wel - come home!

home!   wel-come home!   A wel - come for me!
Wel-come home!   wel-come home!

3 The beautiful gates will unfold, [see;
  The home of the blood-washed I'll
  The city of saints I'll behold!
    For oh! there's a welcome for me!

4 A sinner made whiter than snow,
  I'll join in the mighty acclaim,
  And shout thro' the gates as I go,
    "Salvation to God and the Lamb!"

Dedicated to the Blind Institute of Raleigh, N. C.

No. 156. Jesus, Have Mercy on Me!

P. B. Luke 18: 35-42. P. Bilhorn.

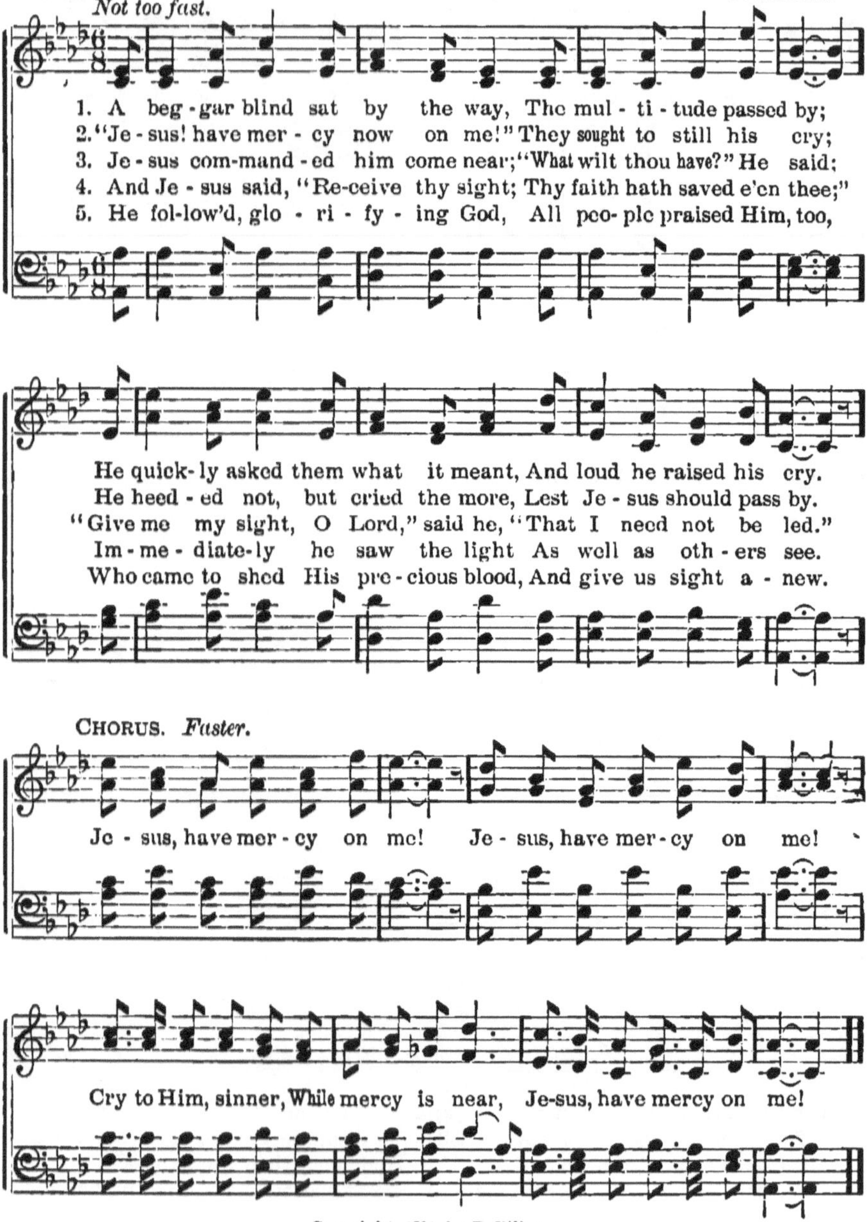
Not too fast.
1. A beg-gar blind sat by the way, The mul-ti-tude passed by;
2. "Je-sus! have mer-cy now on me!" They sought to still his cry;
3. Je-sus com-mand-ed him come near; "What wilt thou have?" He said;
4. And Je-sus said, "Re-ceive thy sight; Thy faith hath saved e'en thee;"
5. He fol-low'd, glo-ri-fy-ing God, All peo-ple praised Him, too,
He quick-ly asked them what it meant, And loud he raised his cry.
He heed-ed not, but cried the more, Lest Je-sus should pass by.
"Give me my sight, O Lord," said he, "That I need not be led."
Im-me-diate-ly he saw the light As well as oth-ers see.
Who came to shed His pre-cious blood, And give us sight a-new.
Chorus. Faster.
Je-sus, have mer-cy on me! Je-sus, have mer-cy on me!
Cry to Him, sinner, While mercy is near, Je-sus, have mercy on me!

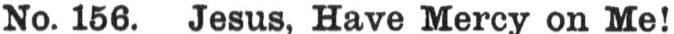

No. 157. All for Jesus.

Mrs. Mary D. James. Mrs. Joseph F. Knapp.

1. All for Je-sus! all for Je-sus! All my be-ing's ransom'd pow'rs;
2. Let my hands perform His bid-ding, Let my feet run in His ways,
3. Since my eyes were fixed on Je-sus, I've lost sight of all be-sides;
4. Oh, what won-der! how a-maz-ing! Je-sus, glo-rious King of kings,

All my tho'ts and words and do-ings, All my days and all my hours.
Let my eyes see Je-sus on-ly, Let my lips speak forth His praise.
So enchain'd my spir-it's vis-ion, Look-ing at the Cru-ci-fied.
Deigns to call me His be-lov-ed, Lets me rest be-neath His wings!

REFRAIN.

All for Je-sus! all for Je-sus! All my days and all my hours.
All for Je-sus! all for Je-sus! Let my lips speak forth His praise.
All for Je-sus! all for Je-sus! Look-ing at the Cru-ci-fied.
All for Je-sus! all for Je-sus! Rest-ing now be-neath His wings!

All for Je-sus! all for Je-sus! All my days and all my hours.
All for Je-sus! all for Je-sus! Let my lips speak forth His praise.
All for Je-sus! all for Je-sus! Look-ing at the Cru-ci-fied.
All for Je-sus! all for Je-sus! Rest-ing now be-neath His wings!

By permission.

No. 158. Whosoever Believeth.

Rev. Frederick Denison.   John 3: 16.   W. Warren Bentley. By per.

1. From Cal-vary's moun-tain sound-ing, What lov-ing words we hear,
2. Oh, seek this great sal-va-tion, And cast out ev-'ry sin,
3. Who-e'er my Word be-liev-eth, We hear the Sav-ior say,
4. O broth-er, come and trust Him, Oh, come to Him to-day,

The love of God a-bound-ing, Dis-pel-ling all our fear.
The soul's e-man-ci-pa-tion, By power Di-vine with-in.
A par-don full re-ceiv-eth, All sins are washed a-way.
He's wait-ing to re-ceive you, Why long-er then de-lay?

REFRAIN.

O broth-er, be-lieve it! O broth-er, re-ceive it!

Who-so-ev-er be-liev-eth Hath ev-er-last-ing life.

NO. 159. Children's Praise.

JULIA H. JOHNSTON.

P. BILHORN.

1. Come, let us sing to the Sav-ior a-bove, Chil-dren a
2. Once in the tem-ple, in joy-ful ac-cord, Chil-dren's ho-
3. Let us re-peat that sweet sto-ry of old, Je-sus the
4. Guard us from dan-ger, and save us from sin, Je-sus, Re-

trib-ute should bring; Sing of His mer-cy and won-der-ful love,
san-nas were heard; Here in His courts we would sing to our Lord,
lit-tle ones blest; Still He is wait-ing in love to en-fold
deem-er and Friend, We are Thy chil-dren, oh, cleanse us with-in.

CHORUS.

He is our Sav-ior and King.   Je - sus, Sav - ior!
We would re-joice in His word.
All who will lean on His breast.
Guide us, and keep to the end.   Bless-ed Je - sus, lov-ing Sav-ior,

Help us Thy prais-es to sing, Show us Thy fa-vor and

teach us Thy way, Thou art our Sav-ior and King.

No. 160.   The Best Friend is Jesus.

P. B.

P. BILHORN.

DUET. Sop. (or Ten.) & Alto.

1. Oh, the best friend to have is Je - sus, When the cares of life up-
2. What a friend I have found in Je - sus! Peace and com - fort to my
3. Tho' I pass thro' the night of sor - row, And the chill - y waves of
4. When at last to our home we gath - er, With the loved ones who have

on you roll; He will heal the wound - ed heart, He will
soul He brings; Lean - ing on His might - y arm, I will
Jor - dan roll, Nev - er need I shrink or fear, For my
gone be - fore, We will sing up - on the shore, Prais - ing

strength and grace im - part; Oh, the best friend to have is Je - sus.
fear no ill or harm; Oh, the best friend to have is Je - sus.
Sav - ior is so near; Oh, the best friend to have is Je - sus.
Him for ev - er - more; Oh, the best friend to have is Je - sus.

The Best Friend is Jesus. Concluded.

CHORUS. *Spirited.*

The best friend to have is Je - - - - sus, The best friend to have is
Je - sus ev -'ry day,

Je - - - - - sus, He will help you when you fall, He will
Je - sus all the way;

hear you when you call; Oh, the best friend to have is Je - sus.

No. 161. Behold! a Stranger.

JOSEPH GRIGG.   H. K. OLIVER.

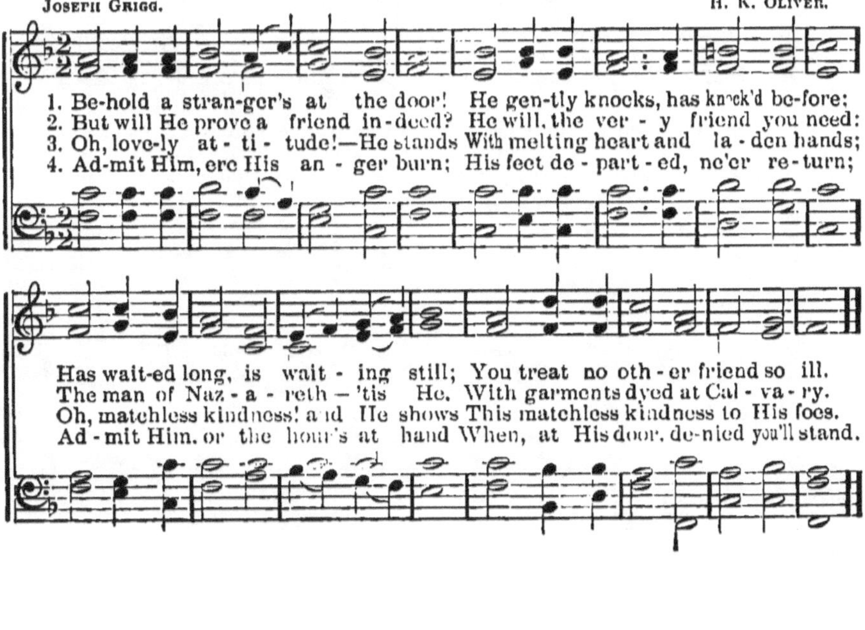

1. Be-hold a stran-ger's at the door! He gen-tly knocks, has knock'd be-fore;
2. But will He prove a friend in-deed? He will, the ver - y friend you need:
3. Oh, love-ly at - ti - tude!—He stands With melting heart and la - den hands;
4. Ad-mit Him, ere His an - ger burn; His feet de - part - ed, ne'er re-turn;

Has wait-ed long, is wait - ing still; You treat no oth - er friend so ill.
The man of Naz - a - reth - 'tis He, With garments dyed at Cal - va - ry.
Oh, matchless kindness! and He shows This matchless kindness to His foes.
Ad - mit Him, or the hour's at hand When, at His door, de-nied you'll stand.

Jesus is Passing This Way.

J. H. T.

1. Is there a sin-ner a-wait-ing Mer-cy and par-don to-day?
2. Broth-er, the Mas-ter is wait-ing, Wait-ing to free-ly for-give;
3. Yes, He is com-ing to bless you While in con-tri-tion you bow:

Wel-come the news that we bring Him, "Je-sus is pass- this way!"
Why not this mo-ment ac-cept Him, Trust in His grace and live?
Com-ing from sin to re-deem you, Read-y to save you now;

Com-ing in love and in mer-cy, Par-don and peace to be-stow,
He is so ten-der and pre-cious, He is so near you to-day;
Can you re-fuse the sal-va-tion Je-sus is of-fer-ing here?

Com-ing to save the poor sin-ner From His heart-anguish and woe.
O-pen your heart to re-ceive Him, While He is pass-ing this way.
O-pen your heart to ad-mit Him, While He is com-ing so near.

CHORUS.

Je-sus is pass-ing this way ... ... To-day ... ... to - day! ...
Je-sus is passing this way. To-day, is pass-ing to-day!

By permission.

Jesus is Passing This Way. Concluded.

While He is near, O be-lieve Him, O-pen your heart to re-ceive Him, For

Je-sus is pass-ing this way, this way, Is passing this way to-day.

No. 163. The Way, the Truth, the Life.

E. R. LATTA.   J. H. T.

1. {"I am the way," the Sav-ior said; The paths of sin for-sake;
   {Slum-ber no more in er-ror's night, In [Omit.] . . . . . .
2. {"I am the truth," the Sav-ior said; In faith draw near to Me;
   {He that be-liev-eth shall be saved, The [Omit.] . . . . . .
3. {"I am the life," the Sav-ior said, Your sins and sor-rows leave;
   {Shun ye the path that leads to death; E-[Omit.] . . . . . .

right-eous-ness a-wake.
truth shall make him free.   } Sinner to-day Hear Jesus say: I am the way, the
ter-nal life re-ceive.

truth, the life, Sinner to-day Hear Jesus say: I am the way, the truth, the life.

By permission.

No. 164.　　　Good News.

When Mr. Moody was first called to preach a funeral sermon, he searched the Bible to find where Jesus had preached sermons of that kind. Instead of finding one, he found that Jesus had turned every funeral He attended from a time of mourning to one of rejoicing, for He said, "I am the Resurrection and the Life." Mr. Moody in referring to this, said; "Is it not good news?" which suggested the words of this hymn.

Arr by P. B.

P. BILHORN.

1. Je - sus died for you and me,
2. It is fin - ished, Je - sus said,
3. From the grave the Sav - ior rose,
4. Now He pleads for us on high,
} Is it not good news?

Now there's par - don full and free,
Sin and death are cap - tive led,
Gain'd the vic - t'ry o'er His foes,
Pleads that we may nev - er die,
} Is it not good news?

On the cross our sins He bore, That on heav'n's e - ter - nal shore,
In the grave our Sav - ior laid, And the last great trib - ute paid,
Christ the law did sat - is - fy, Christ as - cend - ed up on high,
Soon He'll come to claim His own, All who trust in Him a - lone,

We might live for ev - er - more,
Free the sac - ri - fice He made,
We shall meet Him by and by,
We shall gath - er round His throne,
} Is it not good news?

Good News. Concluded.

REFRAIN. *Faster.*

Is it not good news? Is it not good news?

On the cross our sins He bore,
Free the sac - ri - fice He made,
We shall meet Him by and by,
We shall gath - er round His throne,

} Oh, is it not good news?

No. 165. Oh, For a Heart.

Scottish Tune.

1. Oh, for a heart to praise my God, A heart from sin set free!
2. A heart re-signed, sub - miss-ive, meek, My great Re - deem-er's throne;

A heart that al-ways feels Thy blood, So free - ly spilt for me!
Where on - ly Christ is heard to speak; Where Je - sus reigns a - lone.

3 Oh, for a lowly, contrite heart,
    Believing, true, and clean,
  Which neither life nor death can part
    From Him that dwells within!

4 A heart in every thought renewed,
    And full of love divine;
  Perfect and right, and pure and good,
    A copy, Lord, of Thine.

No. 166. A Few More Years of Toil.

J. L. P.

J. L. PATTISON.

Rall.

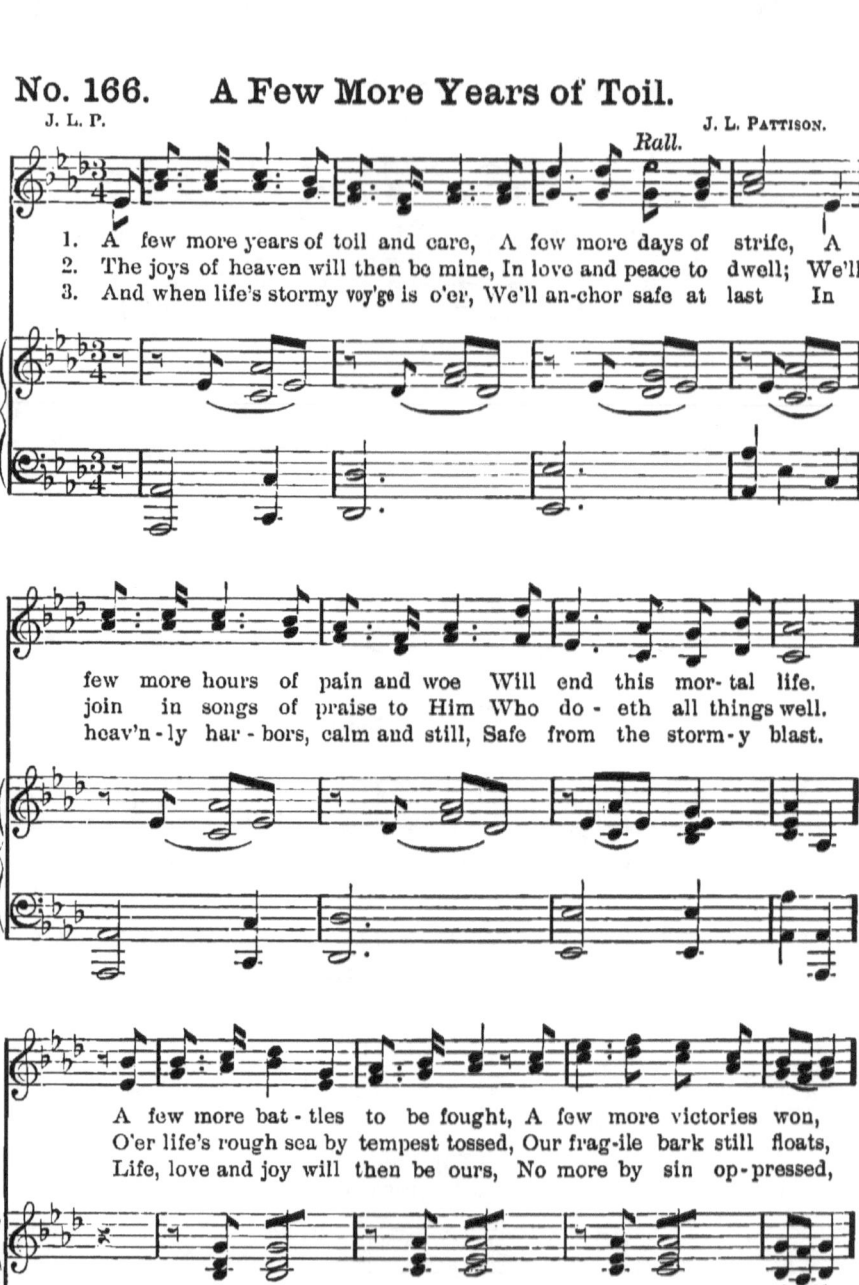

1. A few more years of toil and care, A few more days of strife, A
2. The joys of heaven will then be mine, In love and peace to dwell; We'll
3. And when life's stormy voy'ge is o'er, We'll an-chor safe at last In

few more hours of pain and woe Will end this mor-tal life.
join in songs of praise to Him Who do - eth all things well.
heav'n-ly har - bors, calm and still, Safe from the storm-y blast.

A few more bat - tles to be fought, A few more victories won,
O'er life's rough sea by tempest tossed, Our frag-ile bark still floats,
Life, love and joy will then be ours, No more by sin op-pressed,

A Few More Years of Toil. Concluded.

A few more cross-es to be borne, Then Christ will call us home.
Christ's lov-ing hand is at the helm, He guides our storm-tossed boat.
No more by storm and tem-pest tossed, Our wea - ry souls may rest.

CHORUS.

Trusting in the Lord when the way seems dark, Trusting, ev - er

Rall.

trust-ing, He will guide our bark, Trusting in the Lord when the

storm clouds roll, All will be well with the trust - ing soul.

No. 167. Do you feel your need of Cleansing?

Rev. John McPhail.

M. L. McPhail.

Not too fast.

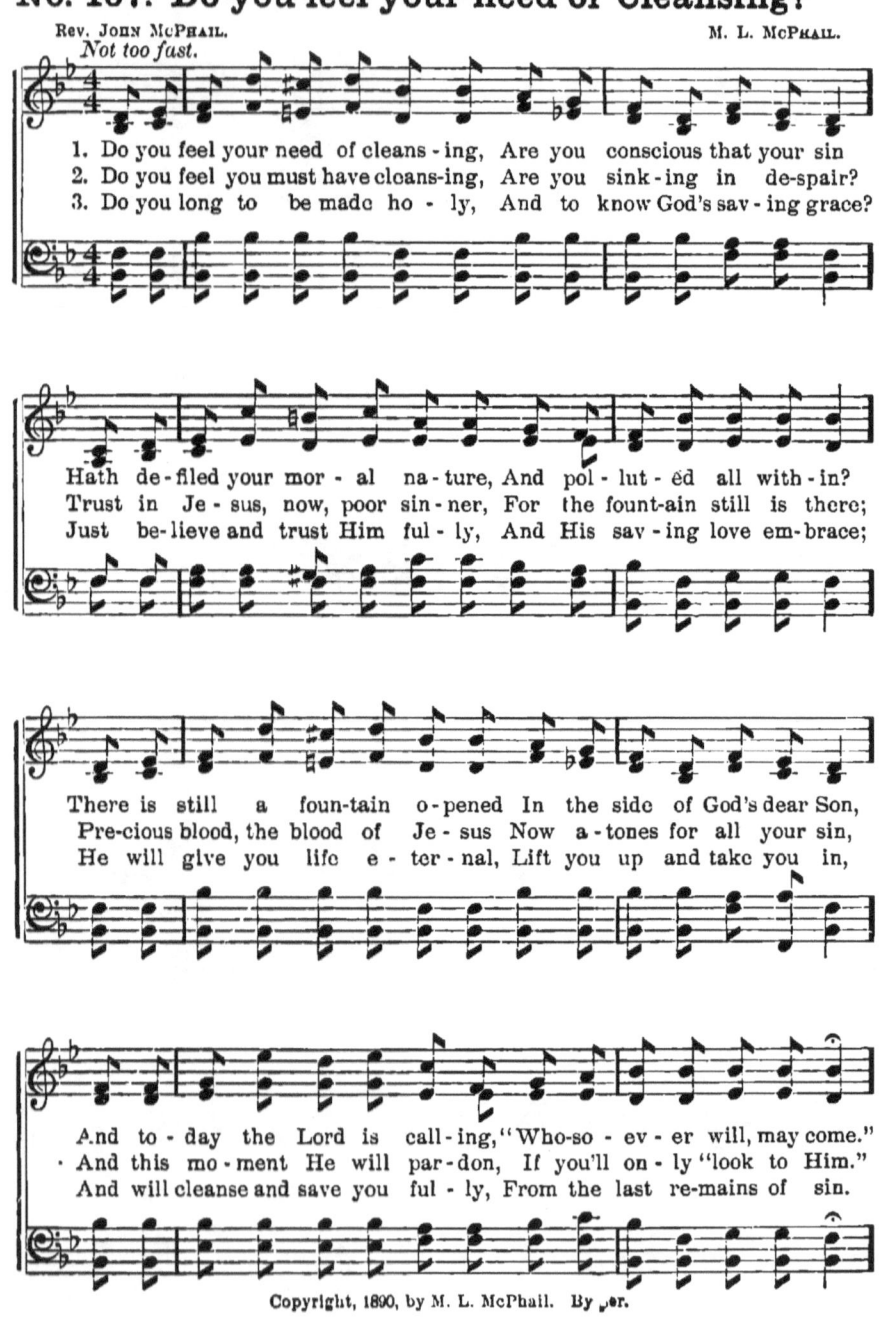

1. Do you feel your need of cleans-ing, Are you conscious that your sin
2. Do you feel you must have cleans-ing, Are you sink-ing in de-spair?
3. Do you long to be made ho-ly, And to know God's sav-ing grace?

Hath de-filed your mor-al na-ture, And pol-lut-ed all with-in?
Trust in Je-sus, now, poor sin-ner, For the fount-ain still is there;
Just be-lieve and trust Him ful-ly, And His sav-ing love em-brace;

There is still a foun-tain o-pened In the side of God's dear Son,
Pre-cious blood, the blood of Je-sus Now a-tones for all your sin,
He will give you life e-ter-nal, Lift you up and take you in,

And to-day the Lord is call-ing, "Who-so-ev-er will, may come."
And this mo-ment He will par-don, If you'll on-ly "look to Him."
And will cleanse and save you ful-ly, From the last re-mains of sin.

Do you feel your need? Concluded.

Then for cleans - ing, pre-cious cleans - ing,
Then for cleansing, pre-cious cleansing, Yes, for cleansing, pre-cious cleansing,

To the foun - tain you may go,
To the foun-tain you may go, to the foun - tain you may go,

And tho' sin - ful And pol - lut - ed,
And tho' sin - ful and pol - lut - ed, tho' sin - ful and pol - lut - ed,

Rit.

Be made whit - er than the snow, than the snow.
Be made whit-er than the snow, Be made whit - er than the snow.

12

No. 168. The Grand Review.

F. A. B.   Matt. 25: 32.   F. A. BLACKMER.

1 Christian sol-dier, worn with serv-ice, Ere dis-charge is grant-ed you,
2 Gird your arm-or on, tho' rust-ed, Soon with use 'twill shine a - new;
3. If you do each du - ty brave-ly, Then the Lord will hon-or you;
4. There'll be glo-ry for the he -roes, Who for God shall here be true,

You must pass Di - vine in-spec-tion At the fi - nal grand re - view.
And in heav-en's strength go for-ward, Ready for the grand re - view.
And your val - or He'll re-mem -ber At the fi - nal grand re - view.
When they're mustered out of serv-ice, And have passed the grand re - view.

CHORUS.

Oh, be watch - - - ful, Christian sol - dier,
watchful, Christian sol - dier, Oh, be watchful, Christian sol-dier,

At your post.....................
At your post stand firm and true, stand firm and true;..................
At your post............... At your post stand firm and true;

Read-y for............... the great in-spec - tion,
Read-y for the great in-spec-tion, Read - y for the great in-spec - tion,

The Grand Review. Concluded.

Read - y for.................... the grand re - view.
for the grand re - view,

No. 169. **Refuge of My Soul.**

Rev. J. B. Dykes.

1. Je - sus, Ref - uge of my soul, Let me to Thy bo - som fly;
2. Oth - er ref - uge have I none, Hangs my help-less soul on Thee;
3. Thou, O Christ, art all I want; More than all in Thee I find;
4. Plenteous grace with Thee is found, Grace to cov - er all my sin;

FINE.

While the near - er wa - ters roll, While the tem-pest still is high,
Leave, oh, leave me not a - lone, Still sup-port and com - fort me;
Raise the fall - en, cheer the faint, Heal the sick, and lead the blind.
Let the heal-ing streams a-bound: Make and keep me pure with - in.

D.S. Safe in - to the hav - en guide, Oh, re-ceive my soul at last.
D.S. Cov - er my de - fense-less head With the shad - ow of Thy wing.
D.S. False and full of sin I am, Thou art full of truth and grace.
D.S. Spring Thou up with - in my heart, Rise to all e - ter - ni - ty.

D. S.

Hide me, O my Sav - ior, hide, Till the storm of life is past;
All my trust on Thee is stayed, All my help from Thee I bring;
Just and ho - ly is Thy name, I am all un-right-eous - ness:
Thou of life the fount - ain art, Free - ly let me take of Thee:

No. 170. Cast All Your Care Upon Him.

The "Lanau." I Peter, 5; 7. P. BILHORN.

1. Oh, why do you car - ry your bur - den a - lone, That
2. Go tell Him your troub - le, He'll give you re - lief, If
3. If sick - ness dis - tress you, or pain, He will heal, Or
4. Then go to Him al - ways, what - ev - er be - fall, Of

bur - den of sor - row and care? Since Je - sus is say - ing in
on Him you'll on - ly de - pend; To cries of His chil - dren He'll
else give you strength to en - dure, To Je - sus who suf - fered, then
sick - ness or sor - row or sin; Tell Je - sus your troub - le, and

ten - der - est tone, Your - self and your bur - den I'll bear.
nev - er be deaf, If on - ly in faith they as - cend.
fer - vent - ly kneel, And trust - ing - ly ask Him to cure.
tell to Him all, And then let your prais - es be - gin.

CHORUS.

Come cast all thy care on Je - sus, Oh, wea - ry and troub - led soul, Come

cast all thy bur - den up - on Him; He wants not a part but the whole.

No. 171. Leaning on the Everlasting Arms.

Rev. E. A. Hoffman. Deut. 33: 27. A. J. Showalter.

1. What a fel-low-ship, what a joy di-vine, Lean-ing on the ev-er-
2. Oh, how sweet to walk in this pil-grim way, Lean-ing on the ev-er-
3. What have I to dread, what have I to fear, Lean-ing on the ev-er-

last-ing Arms, What a bless-ed-ness, what a peace is mine,
last-ing Arms, Oh, how bright the path grows from day to day,
last-ing Arms? I have bless-ed peace with my Lord so near,

Lean-ing on the ev-er-last-ing Arms. Lean - - - ing,
Lean-ing on Je-sus,

lean - - - ing, Safe and se-cure from all a-larms, Lean - ing,
lean-ing on Je-sus, Leaning on Je-sus,

lean - - - ing, Lean-ing on the ev-er-last-ing Arms.
lean-ing on Je-sus,

No. 172. Standing on the Promises.

R. K. C.

R. KELSO CARTER.

1. Stand-ing on the prom-is-es of Christ, my King, Thro' e - ter - nal a - ges let His prais-es ring; Glo-ry in the high-est, I will shout and sing,
2. Stand-ing on the prom-is-es that can not fail, When the howl-ing storms of doubt and fear as - sail, By the liv-ing Word of God I shall pre-vail,
3. Stand-ing on the prom-is-es, I now can see Per - fect, pres-ent cleansing in the blood for me; Standing in the lib - er - ty where Christ makes free,
4. Stand-ing on the prom-is-es of Christ, the Lord, Bound to Him e-ter - nal-ly by love's strong cord, O-ver-coming dai - ly with the Spir-it's sword,
5. Stand-ing on the prom-is-es, I can not fall, List-'ning ev - ery mo-ment to the Spir-it's call; Rest-ing in my Sav-ior as my all in all,

CHORUS.

Stand - ing, stand - ing,

Standing on the promises of God. Standing on the promise, standing on the promise,

Stand - ing,

Stand-ing on the prom-is-es of God, my Sav - ior; Standing on the promise,

Standing on the Promises. Concluded.

Stand - - - - ing,

Stand-ing on the prom-ise, I'm stand-ing on the prom-is-es of God.

No. 173. Sing Unto the Lord.

Miss Ada Blenkhorn.   P. Bilhorn.

1. Come, let us sing un - to the Lord, He washed us in His precious blood,
2. His wondrous love come let us sing, As joy - ous as the birds in Spring;
3. Come, let us join the ransomed throng, And sing with joy the glad, new song;

FINE.

And made us kings and priests to God; All praise to Christ, our Lord.
And let each strain with glad-ness ring, Oh, sing un - to the Lord.
The sweet-est notes to Him be - long, Oh, sing un - to the Lord.

D.S. Oh, let His prais - es day by day Our hearts and lips em - ploy.
D.S. His ho - ly words of match-less power E - ter - nal life im - part.
D.S. To Him who, with a robe and crown, A - waits us in the skies.

D. S.

He fills our souls with per - fect peace, Our sor - row turns to joy;
His prom - is - es are tried and true, To ev - ery trust - ing heart
Our prayers of faith and songs of praise, Like in - cense sweet, shall rise

No. 174. Glory to God, 'tis Jesus.

Miss Julia H. Johnston.

P. Bilhorn.

1. Who can heal a troub-led soul?
2. Who has pow'r to cleanse from sin?
3. Who has pow'r the lost to save?
4. Who has grace for ev - 'ry hour?
5. Who can drive a - way all fear?
6. Who can keep us all the way?
} Glo - ry to God, 'tis Je - sus;

Who can make the sin - ner whole?
Who re - news the heart with - in?
Who can ran - som from the grave?
Who can foil the tempt-er's pow'r?
Who can bring re - lief and cheer?
Bring us to the crown-ing day?
} Glo - ry to God, 'tis Je - sus.

CHORUS.

Glo - ry to God, He saved my soul; Glo - ry to God, He makes me whole;

Glo - ry to God, He'll save your soul, Glo - ry to God, 'tis Je - sus.

No. 175.　The Half has Never Been Told.

FRANCES R. HAVERGAL.

R. E. HUDSON.

1. I know I love Thee bet-ter, Lord, Than an-y earth-ly joy,
2. I know that Thou art near-er still Than an-y earth-ly throng,
3. Thou hast put glad-ness in my heart; Then well may I be glad!
4. O Sav-ior, pre-cious Sav-ior mine! What will Thy pres-ence be,

For Thou hast giv-en me the peace Which noth-ing can de-stroy.
And sweet-er is the tho't of Thee Than an-y love-ly song.
With-out the se-cret of Thy love I could not but be sad.
If such a life of joy can crown Our walk on earth with Thee?

CHORUS.

The half has nev-er yet been told, (yet been told,) Of love so full and free; The half has nev-er yet been told, (yet been told,) The blood— it cleans-eth me, (clean-eth me.)

Rit.

No. 176. The Lord's our Rock!

V. J. C. P. BILHORN.

1. The Lord's our Rock, in Him we hide; A shel-ter in the time of storm!
2. A shade by day, de-fence by night, A shel-ter in the time of storm!
3. The rag-ing storm may round us beat, A shel-ter in the time of storm!
4. O Rock di-vine, O Ref-uge dear, A shel-ter in the time of storm!

Se - cure what-ev - er ill be - tide, A shel-ter in the time of storm!
No fears a - larm, no foes af - fright, A shel-ter in the time of storm!
We'll nev - er leave our safe re - treat, A shel-ter in the time of storm!
Be Thou our Help-er, ev - er near, A shel-ter in the time of storm!

CHORUS.

Oh, Je - sus is the Rock in a wea - ry land, A wea - ry land, a wea - ry land, Oh, Je - sus is the Rock in a wea - ry land, A shel - ter in the time of storm.

Copyright, 1891, by P. Bilhorn.

No. 177. Jesus, Take Me In.

JOHN WILLAN. JOHN WILLAN.

1. Have mer - cy on me, Je - sus, And wash a - way my sin;
2. I long to be for - giv - en, And know that I am Thine;
3. I know I'm vile and sin - ful, And oft - en full of doubt;
4. Re - mem - ber Thy rich pro - mise, Re - mem - ber Cal - va - ry,
5. Oh, yes, lost one, I'll take you, For such I came to save;

I'm lost, but oh, my Sav - ior, Wilt Thou not take me in?
Oh, let me now come to Thee, And take this heart of mine.
But yet I must come to Thee, Oh, do not cast me out!
And let a poor, lost sin - ner Take shel - ter, Lord, in Thee.
I long for you have wait - ed, Now look, be - lieve and live.

CHORUS.

Je - sus, take me in, Je - sus, take me in!

Cho. for last verse.

I will take you in, I will take you in:

Rit.

I'm lost, but oh, my Sav - ior, Wilt Thou not take me in?
You're lost, but I will save you, And free - ly take you in.

Copyright, 1889, by John Willan. By per.

No. 178. Soldiers in the Army.

Rev. J. McPhail.   M. L. McPhail.

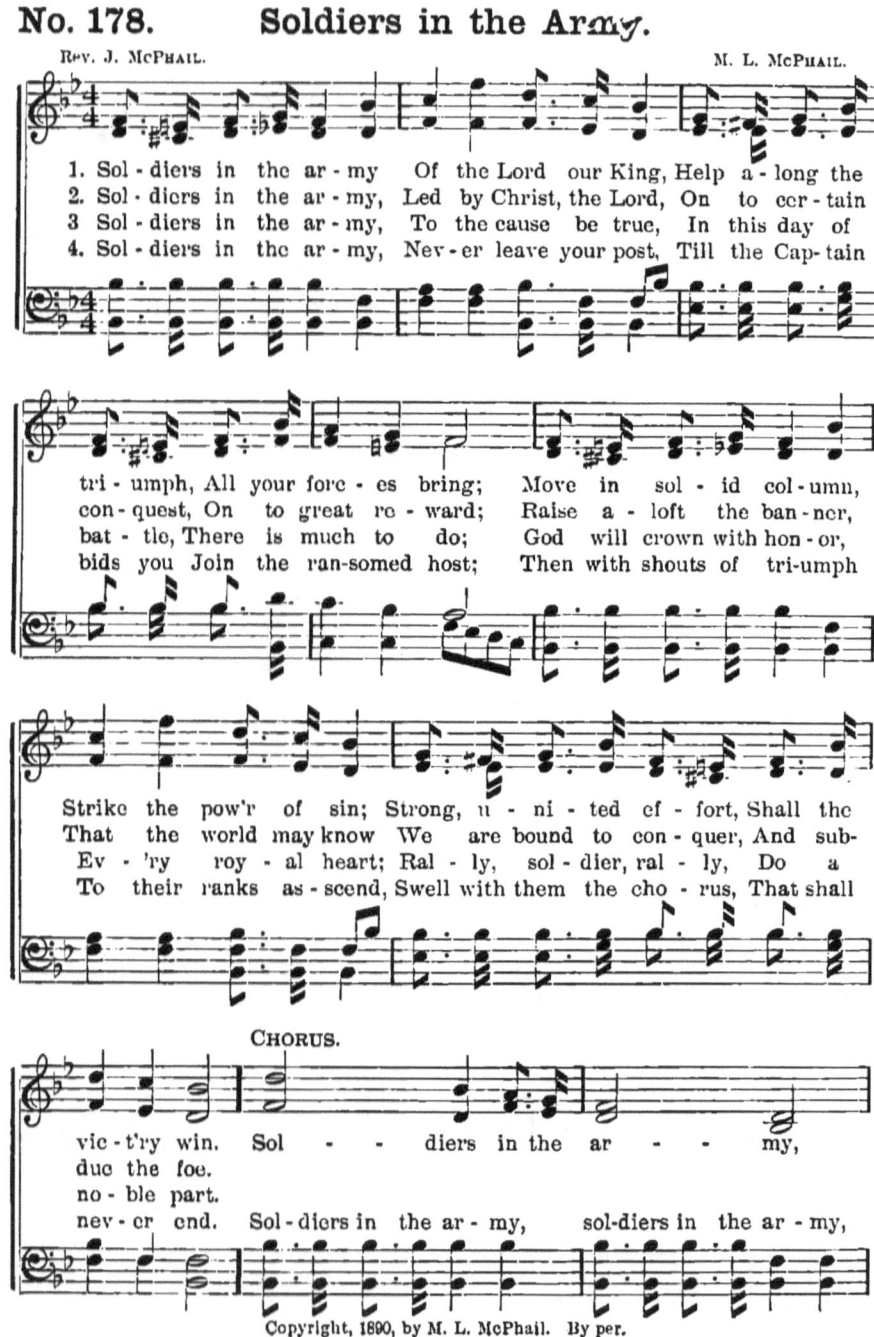

1. Sol - diers in the ar - my Of the Lord our King, Help a - long the
2. Sol - diers in the ar - my, Led by Christ, the Lord, On to cer - tain
3. Sol - diers in the ar - my, To the cause be true, In this day of
4. Sol - diers in the ar - my, Nev - er leave your post, Till the Cap - tain

tri - umph, All your forc - es bring; Move in sol - id col - umn,
con - quest, On to great re - ward; Raise a - loft the ban - ner,
bat - tle, There is much to do; God will crown with hon - or,
bids you Join the ran - somed host; Then with shouts of tri - umph

Strike the pow'r of sin; Strong, u - ni - ted ef - fort, Shall the
That the world may know We are bound to con - quer, And sub -
Ev - 'ry roy - al heart; Ral - ly, sol - dier, ral - ly, Do a
To their ranks as - cend, Swell with them the cho - rus, That shall

CHORUS.

vic - t'ry win. Sol - diers in the ar - my,
due the foe.
no - ble part.
nev - er end. Sol - diers in the ar - my, sol - diers in the ar - my,

Soldiers in the Army. Concluded.

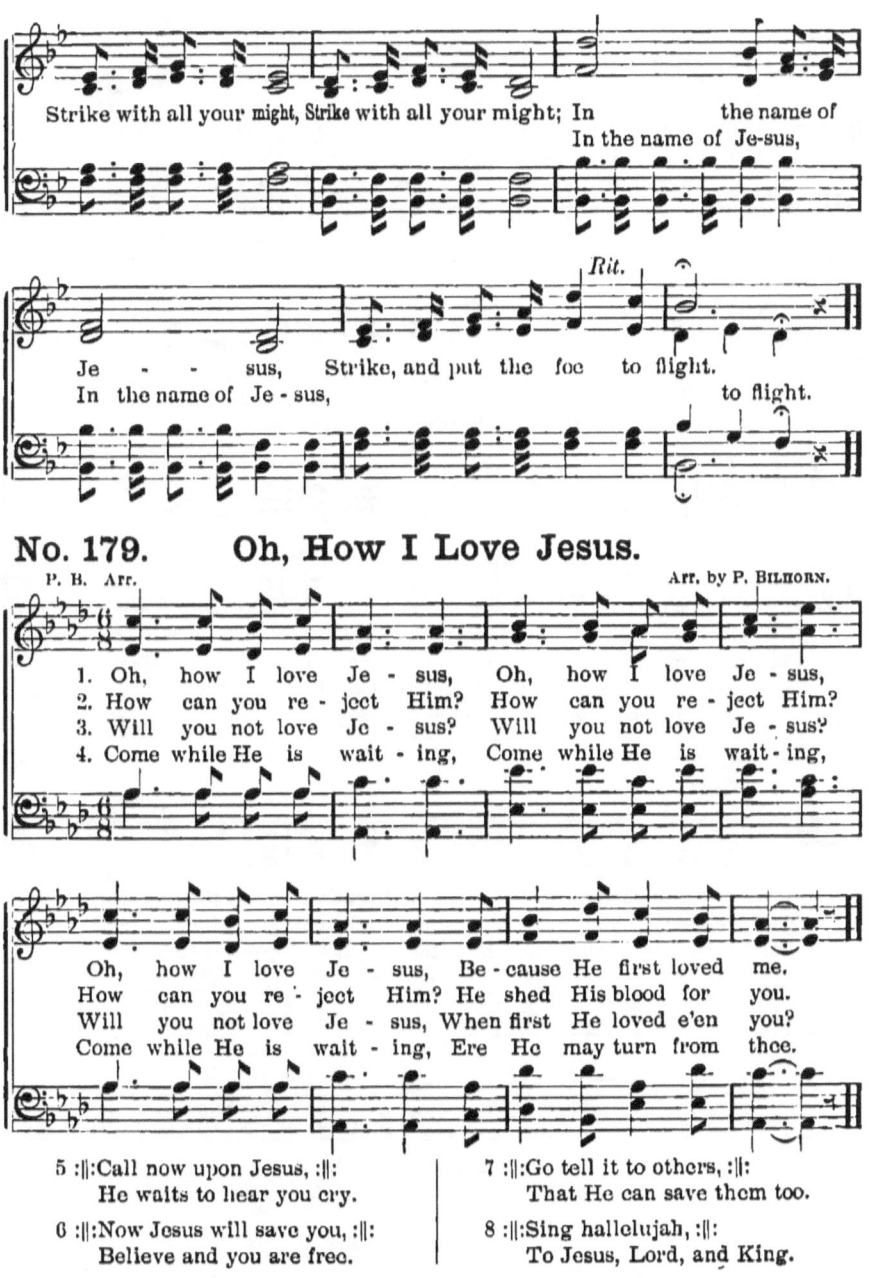

Strike with all your might, Strike with all your might; In the name of
In the name of Je-sus,

Je - - sus, Strike, and put the foe to flight.
In the name of Je - sus, to flight.

Rit.

No. 179. Oh, How I Love Jesus.

P. B. Arr.   Arr. by P. Bilhorn.

1. Oh, how I love Je - sus, Oh, how I love Je - sus,
2. How can you re - ject Him? How can you re - ject Him?
3. Will you not love Je - sus? Will you not love Je - sus?
4. Come while He is wait - ing, Come while He is wait - ing,

Oh, how I love Je - sus, Be - cause He first loved me.
How can you re - ject Him? He shed His blood for you.
Will you not love Je - sus, When first He loved e'en you?
Come while He is wait - ing, Ere He may turn from thee.

5 :‖:Call now upon Jesus, :‖:
   He waits to hear you cry.

6 :‖:Now Jesus will save you, :‖:
   Believe and you are free.

7 :‖:Go tell it to others, :‖:
   That He can save them too.

8 :‖:Sing hallelujah, :‖:
   To Jesus, Lord, and King.

No. 180. Light will Greet Thee By and By.

Latta C. Lord.   L. B. Shook.

1. Is thy trembling heart a-wea-ry? Are thy foot-steps al-most gone?
2. Is thy spir-it sad with-in thee? Raise thy heart in earn-est prayer,
3. Has thy spir-it grown a-wea-ry? Do not fal-ter in the strife,

Does life seem a bur-den drear-y? Cour-age, broth-er, strug-gle on,
Just a Fa-ther's lov-ing kind-ness, Trust a Fa-ther's ten-der care;
God has worked for thee, my broth-er, As thou treadst the path of life;

Bear it pa-tient-ly and brave-ly, Do not stop to weep or sigh,
Call up-on Him in thy sor-row, He will hear thy fal-t'ring cry,
Darkness may ob-scure thy path-way, Clouds may gather in thy sky,

Af-ter night the morn-ing dawneth, Light will greet thee by and by.
Tho' thou scest no sign of dawn-ing, Light will greet thee by and by.
Storms may rage, but do not fal-ter, Light will greet thee by and by.

CHORUS.

By and by.......... the morn-ing dawn - - eth, By and
By and by   the morning dawns,

Light will Greet Thee. Concluded.

by,........ yes, by and by,   Tho' thou seest...... no sings of
By and by,   yes, by and by,   Tho' thou seest,

dawn - - - ing, Light will greet....... thee by and by.
no signs of dawn,   Light will greet thee by and by, yes, by and by.

No. 181.   A Sinner Like Me.

C. J. B.   CHAS. J. BUTLER.

1. I was once far away from the Savior, And as vile as a sinner could be,
2. I wan-dered on in the darkness, Not a ray of light could I see,
3. And then in that dark lonely hour, A voice sweetly whispered to me,
4. I then ful-ly trust-ed in Je-sus, And oh, what a joy came to me!

I wondered if Christ the Redeemer Could save a poor sinner like me.
And the tho't filled my heart with sadness, There's no hope for a sinner like me.
Saying Christ the Redeemer has pow-er To save a poor sinner like me.
My heart He filled with His praises, And saved such a sinner like me.

5 No longer in darkness I'm walking,
  For His light is now shining in me.
And now unto others I'm telling,
  How He saves a poor sinner like me.

6 Then listen, poor wandering sinner,
  To a message so tender and true,
That Christ, the dear loving Savior,
  Is willing to save even you.

No. 182. Is There One Prepared for Me?

Harry Clayton.

1. Man-sions are pre-pared a - bove, By the gra - cious God of Love;
2. Crowns that daz-zle hu - man eye, Wait for those who reach the sky,
3. Robes of spot - less white are giv'n, By the gra - cious King of heav'n,
4. Harps of sol - emn sound a - bove, Swell loud prais - es to His love;

Ma - ny will those man - sions see; Is there one pre-pared for me?
Ma - ny will those bright crowns be, Is there one pre-pared for me?
All can have them, they are free, Is there one pre-pared for me?
Oh, how sweet this sound will be, Is there one pre-pared for me?

REFRAIN.

Is there one pre-pared for me?
Is there one........... pre-pared for me? Is there

Is there one pre-pared for me?
one................ pre-pared for me?

1. Ma - ny
2. Ma - ny
3. All can
4. Oh, how

Is There One Prepared? Concluded.

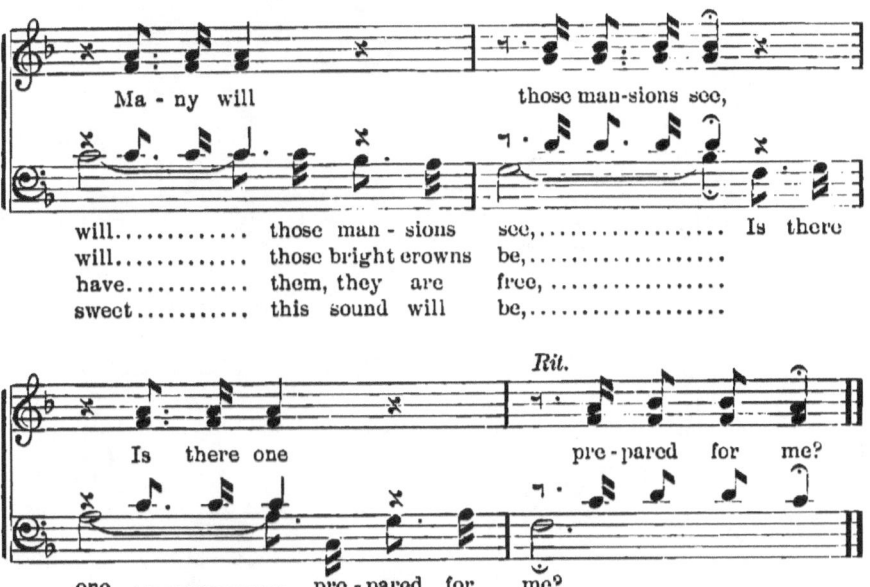

Ma-ny will those man-sions see,

will............ those man-sions see,................ Is there
will............ those bright crowns be,....................
have........... them, they are free, ...
sweet.......... this sound will be,................

Rit.

Is there one pre-pared for me?

one................ pre-pared for me?

No. 183. Hamburg. L. M.

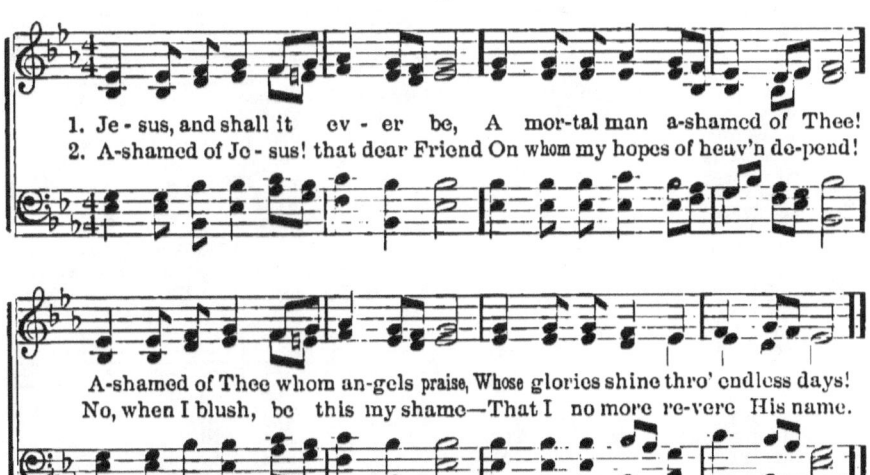

1. Je - sus, and shall it ev - er be, A mor-tal man a-shamed of Thee!
2. A-shamed of Je - sus! that dear Friend On whom my hopes of heav'n de-pend!

A-shamed of Thee whom an-gels praise, Whose glories shine thro' endless days!
No, when I blush, be this my shame—That I no more re-vere His name.

3 Ashamed of Jesus! yes I may,
When I've no guilt to wash away;
No tear to wipe, no good to crave,
No fears to quell, no soul to save.

4 Till then—nor is my boasting vain—
Till then, I boast a Savior slain;
And oh, may this my glory be—
That Christ is not ashamed of me.

No. 184. Let Me Rest.

Dr. H. Bonar.　　　　　　　　　　　　　　　　H. N. Lincoln. By per.

1. In the shad-ow of the Rock　let me　rest,........... When I
2. On the parch'd and des-ert way　where I　tread.......... With the
3. I in peace will rest me here　till I　see .... That the

1. In the shadow of the Rock let me
2. On the parch'd and des-ert way where I tread
3. I in peace will rest me here till I see, till I see That the

feel the tem-pest's shock　thrill my breast,　　　All in
scorch-ing noon-tide ray　o'er my head,　　　Let me
skies a-gain are fair　o-ver me,　　　That the

rest,.....................When I feel the tem-pest's shock thrill my
　　　　With the scorch-ing noon-tide ray　o'er my head,
skies a-gain are fair　o-ver me,　o-ver me, That the

vain the storm shall sweep　while I　hide,....................
find a wel-come shade　cool and　still,...................
burn-ing heats are past　and the　day ....

breast,........................ All in vain the storm shall sweep
　　　Let me find a wel-come shade cool and still,
burn-ing heats are past and the day, and the day

And my tran-quil vig-il keep　by Thy side.
And my wea-ry steps be stayed　by Thy will.
Bids the trav-el-er at last　go His way.

While I hide...................... by Thy side............
Bids the trav-el-er at last go His way, go His way.

Let Me Rest. Concluded.

CHORUS.

In the shad-ow of the Rock let me rest, In the

shad-ow of the Rock let me rest, When I feel the tem-pest's

shock thrill my breast. In the shad-ow of the Rock let me rest.

No. 185. Stand up and Bless the Lord.

By per.

1. Stand up and bless the Lord, Ye peo-ple of His choice;
2. Tho' high a-bove all praise, A-bove all bless-ing high,
3. Oh, for the liv-ing flame From His own al-tar brought,

Stand up, and bless the Lord your God, With heart, and soul, and voice.
Who would not fear His ho-ly name, And laud, and mag-ni-fy?
To touch our lips, our souls in-spire, And wing to heaven our thought.

No. 186. Standing by the Cross.

ALLEN SHIRLEY Ref. by A. J. S. A. J. SHOWALTER.

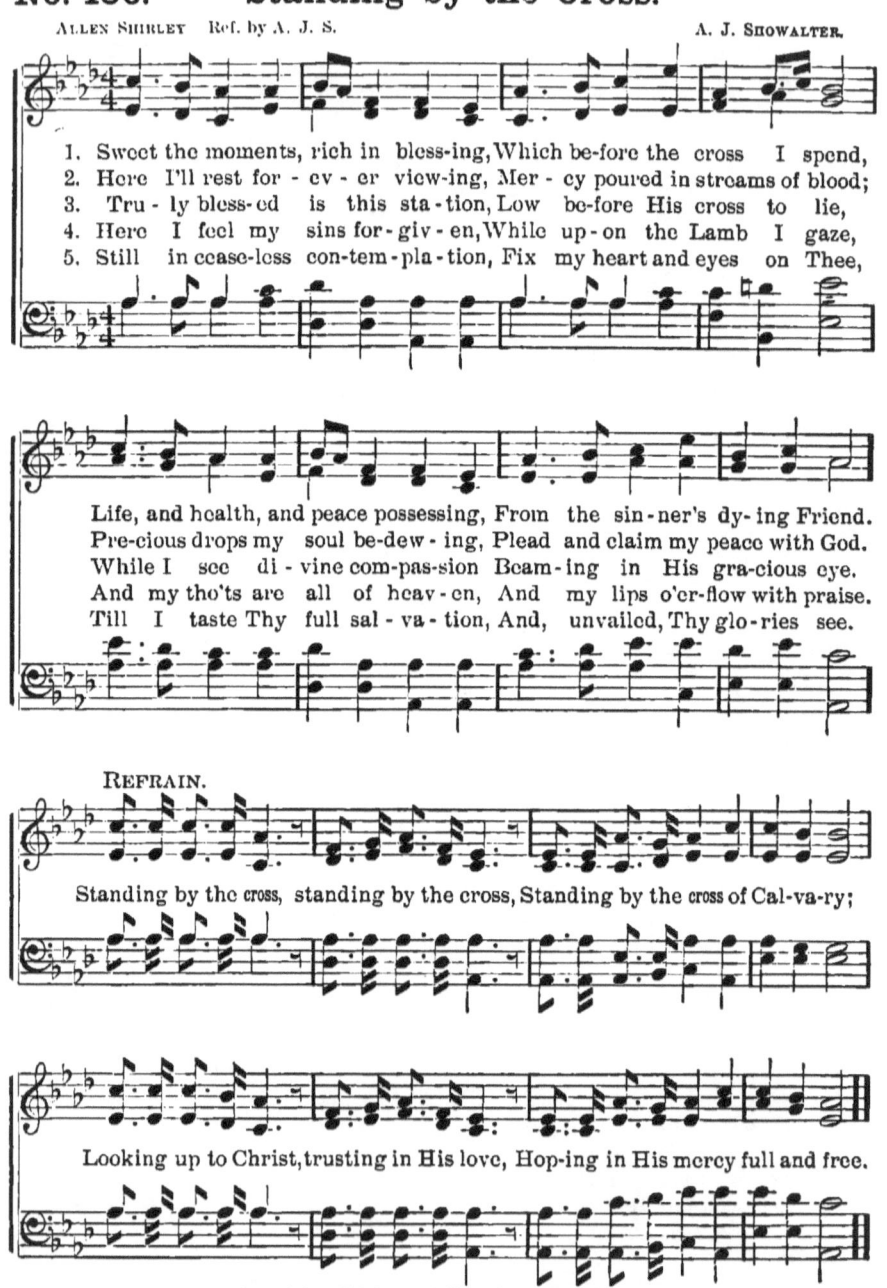

1. Sweet the moments, rich in bless-ing, Which be-fore the cross I spend,
2. Here I'll rest for - ev - er view-ing, Mer - cy poured in streams of blood;
3. Tru - ly bless-ed is this sta - tion, Low be-fore His cross to lie,
4. Here I feel my sins for-giv - en, While up - on the Lamb I gaze,
5. Still in cease-less con-tem-pla-tion, Fix my heart and eyes on Thee,

Life, and health, and peace possessing, From the sin-ner's dy-ing Friend.
Pre-cious drops my soul be-dew - ing, Plead and claim my peace with God.
While I see di - vine com-pas-sion Beam-ing in His gra-cious eye.
And my tho'ts are all of heav - en, And my lips o'er-flow with praise.
Till I taste Thy full sal - va - tion, And, unvailed, Thy glo-ries see.

REFRAIN.

Standing by the cross, standing by the cross, Standing by the cross of Cal-va-ry;

Looking up to Christ, trusting in His love, Hop-ing in His mercy full and free.

Copyright, 1891, by A. J. Showalter. Used by per.

No. 187. He Hideth My Soul.

FANNY J. CROSBY. WM. J. KIRKPATRICK. By per.

Allegretto.

1. A won-der-ful Sav-ior is Je-sus my Lord, A won-der-ful
2. A won-der-ful Sav-ior is Je-sus my Lord, He tak-eth my
3. With num-ber-less bless-ings each mo-ment He crowns; And filled with His
4. When clothed in His brightness trans-port-ed I rise To meet Him in

Sav-ior to me; He hid-eth my soul in the cleft of the rock, Where
bur-den a - way; He hold-eth me up, and I shall not be moved, He
full-ness di - vine, I sing in my rap-ture O glo-ry to God For
clouds of the sky; His per-fect sal - va-tion, His won-der-ful love, I'll

CHORUS.

riv-ers of pleas-ure I see.
giv-eth me strength as my day. } He hideth my soul in the cleft of the rock,
such a Re-deem-er as mine!
shout with the millions on high.

That shadows a dry, thirst-y land; He hid-eth my life in the depths of His

love, And covers my head with His hand, And cov-ers my head with His hand.

Copyright, 1890, by Wm. J. Kirkpatrick.

No. 188. Trust and Follow On.

Rev. H. B. TOWNSEND. P. BILHORN.

1. The way may be thorn-lined and pain-ful to tread, But
2. The night may be dark and no stars o - ver-head, We may
3. Death's riv - er may roll its cold wave at our feet, We may
4. O ye who are grop - ing in dark - ness and sin, 'Tis the

we have been called to o - bey, So with Je - sus we'll walk, of sal-
stum - ble and fall tho' we pray; But our Guide safe - ly leads, and sup-
come to the close of the day; Yet no e - vil we fear, for our
Sav - ior is call - ing to - day; He is will - ing to save you and

va - tion we'll talk, As we trust and go on in the way.
plies all our needs, As we trust and go on in the way.
Je - sus is near, As we trust and go on in the way.
cleanse you with - in, If you'll trust and go on in the way.

CHORUS.

Then we'll trust and go on in the way, Trust - ing the
Sav - ior each day; Our cross - es He'll bear, And our

Trust and Follow On. Concluded.

sor - rows He'll share, As we trust and go on in the way.

No. 189.   When the King Comes in.

J. E. LANDOR.   E. S. LORENZ.

1. Call'd to the feast by the King are we, Sit-ting, perhaps, where His
2. Crowns on the head where the thorns have been, Glo-ri-fied He who once
3. Like lightning's flash will that instant show Things hidden long from both
4. Joy-ful His eye shall on each one rest Who is in white wedding

peo - ple   be: How will it   fare, then, with thee and me,
died for men;   Splen-did the vis - ion be - fore us then,
friend and foe, Just what we are   ev - 'ry one will know,
gar-ments dressed—Ah! well for us   if   we stand the test,

REFRAIN.

When the King comes in? When the King comes in, brother, When the King comes

in!   How will it fare with thee and me When the King comes in?

From "Songs of Grace." By per.

No. 190. Tell it Out!

F. R. HAVERGAL.　　　　　　　　　　　　　　　　　　　P. BILHORN.

1. Tell it out a - mong the na - tions that the Lord is King;
2. Tell it out a - mong the peo - ple that the Sav - ior reigns;
3. Tell it out a - mong the peo - ple, Je - sus reigns a - bove;

Tell it out! (tell it out!) Tell it out! (tell it out!) Tell it

out a-mong the na-tions, bid them shout and sing;
out a-mong the hea-then, bid them break their chains; Tell it out! (tell it out!)
out a-mong the na-tions that His reign is love;

Tell it out! (tell it out!
Tell it out with ad - o - ra - tion that He
Tell it out a - mong the weep-ing ones that
Tell it out a - mong the high-ways and the

shall in-crease, That the might - y King of glo - ry is the
Je - sus lives, Tell it out a - mong the wea - ry ones what
lanes at home, Let it ring a - cross the mount-ains and the

Tell it Out! Concluded.

King of peace; Tell it out with ju - bi - la - tion, let the
rest He gives, Tell it out a - mong the sin - ners that He
o - cean's foam, That the wea - ry, heav - y - la - den need no

song ne'er cease; }
came to save; } Tell it out! (tell it out!) Tell it out! (tell it out!)
long - er roam; }

No. 191. 'Tis the Old Time Religion.

Old Folks.   Arr. by P. Bilhorn.

CHO.—'Tis the old time re - lig - ion, 'Tis the old time re - lig - ion,
1. It was good for our fa - thers, It was good for our moth - ers,
2. Makes me love ev - 'ry bod - y, Makes me love ev - 'ry bod - y,
3. It will save a poor, lost sin - ner, It will save a poor, lost sin - ner,

'Tis the old time re - lig - ion, And 'tis good e - nough for me.
It was good for our broth-ers, And 'tis good e - nough for me.
Makes me love ev - 'ry bod - y, And 'tis good e - nough for me.
It will save a poor, lost sin - ner, And 'tis good e - nough for me.

4 :||:It was good for the prophet Daniel,:||:   6 :||:It will do when we are dying,:||:
   And 'tis good enough for me.   And 'tis good enough for me.

5 :||:It was good for Paul and Silas,:||:   7 :||:It will take us home to heaven,:||:
   And 'tis good enough for me.   And 'tis good enough for me.

No. 192.

Which Side?

FRANCES R. HAVERGAL.

A. J. SHOWALTER.

1. Who is on the Lord's side? Who will serve the King?
2. Je - sus, Thou hast bought us, Not with gold or gem,
3. Fierce must be the con - flict, Strong may be the foe,
4. Cho - sen to be sol - diers In an al - ien land,

Who will be His help - ers, Oth - er lives to bring?
But with Thine own life - blood, For Thy di - a - dem;
But the King's own ar - my None may o - ver - throw;
Cho - sen, called and faith - ful For our Cap - tain's band;

Who will leave the world's side? Who will face the foe? Who is on the
With Thy bless - ing fill - ing Each who comes to Thee, Thou hast made us
Round His stand - ard rang - ing Vic - t'ry is se - cure. For His truth un -
In the serv - ice roy - al, Let us not grow cold, Let us be right

D. S. *By Thy call of mer - cy, By Thy grace di - vine, We are on the*

Rit. FINE. CHORUS.

Lord's side? Who for Him will go? ⎫
will - ing, Thou hast made us free. ⎪
chang - ing Makes the tri - umph sure. ⎬ By Thy call of mer - cy,
loy - al, No - ble, true and bold. ⎭

Lord's side, Sav - ior, we are Thine.

By permission.

Which Side? Concluded.

D. S.

By Thy grace di-vine, We are on the Lord's side, Sav-ior, we are Thine.

No. 193.   The Gospel Railroad.

Mrs. Hall Booth.   H. H. Booth. Arr. by P. Bilhorn.

1. The road to heav'n thro' Christ was laid, With precious blood the rails are made;
2. Re - pent-ance is   the sta-tion, then, Where pas-sen-gers are tak - en   in;
3. The Bi - ble is   the en - gi - neer, It points the way to heav'n so clear;
4. God's love the fire, His truth the steam, Which drives the en-gine and the train;

From earth to heav'n the line ex-tends, To life e - ter - nal where it ends.
No fee for them is then to pay, For Je - sus is Him-self the way.
Thro' tun-nels dark, and drear-y here, It does the way to glo - ry steer.
All you who would to glo - ry ride, Must come to Christ, in Him a - bide.

CHORUS. *Repeat p.*   *ff*

I'm go-ing home, I'm go-ing home, I'm go-ing home to die no more.
To die no more, to die no more, I'm go-ing home to die no more.

5 Come, then, poor sinner, now's the
  At any station on the line;   [time,
  If you repent and turn from sin,
  The train will stop and take you in.

6 And then to glory we will go,
  With all on board as white as snow;
  So ring the bell, and start the train,
  And run it through in Jesus' name.

No. 194. I'll Enter the Open Door.

Moderato.

A. J. SHOWALTER.

1. I have long'd for the bliss of par - don, And sigh'd to be cleans'd from sin,
2. I will trust tho' I walk in dark-ness, And pray till the light I see,
3. I have long'd for the bliss of par - don, And sigh'd to be cleans'd from sin,

And I know if I come be - liev - ing My Sav - ior will let me in.
For the blood that will cleanse the vil - est Will sure - ly a - vail for me.
And I knock at the door be - liev - ing That Je - sus will let me in.

For the door of His love is o - pen, He wait- eth for those who seek,
I have on - ly the plea to of - fer, That Je - sus for me has died,
Oh, the faith in my soul grows stronger, I trem - ble with fear no more,

But I trem - ble with fear and doubting, Oh, why is my faith so weak?
And with on - ly my heart to give Him, I haste to His bless - ed side.
'Tis my Sav - ior that bids me wel-come, I'll en - ter the o - pen door.

I'll Enter the Open Door. Concluded.

CHORUS.

I'll en-ter the o-pen door, I'll en-ter the o-pen door,
wide o-pen door, wide o-pen door,

'Tis Je-sus in-vites, I'll en-ter in, I'll en-ter the o-pen door.

No. 195. Do I not Need Thee?

R. G. STAPLES.   John 15: 5.   H. N. LINCOLN.

1. Do I not need Thee, Sav - ior di - vine! To Thy dear pre-cepts
2. Do I not need Thee, Each hour, each day! Pit-y me, Sav-ior,
3. Do I not need Thee! What pow'r have I! No arm to lean on,

CHORUS.

My heart in-cline. }
Be Thou my stay. } How much I need Thee, I scarce-ly know;
Sav - ior, draw nigh. }

Dear, pre-cious Sav-ior, Thy love be-stow.

4 Do I not need Thee!
  Weary and faint,
  Come I unto Thee,
  Heed my complaint.

5 Yes! I do need Thee,
  Thy love is strong;
  Give me to praise Thee,
  In endless song.

No. 196. Calling the Prodigal.

C. H. G.

CHAS. H. GABRIEL.

1. God is call-ing the prod-i-gal, come with-out de-lay,
2. Pa-tient, lov-ing, and ten-der-ly still the Fa-ther pleads,
3. Come, there's bread in the house of thy Fa-ther, and to spare,

Hear, oh, hear Him call-ing, call-ing now for thee......
Hear, oh, hear Him call-ing, call-ing now for thee......
Hear, oh, hear Him call-ing, call-ing now for thee......

for thee.

Though you've wan-dered so far from His pres-ence, come to-day,
Oh! re-turn while the spir-it in mer-cy in-ter-cedes,
Lo! the ta-ble is spread and the feast is wait-ing there,

CHORUS.

Hear His loving voice calling still......... Call - - - ing now for
calling still. Calling now for thee,

Calling the Prodigal. Concluded.

thee,............. Oh, wea - - - - - - - - ry prod-i-gal,
call-ing now for thee, Wea-ry prod - i - gal, come,

come............. Call - - - - ing now for thee,............
wea-ry prod-i-gal, come, Call-ing now for thee, call-ing now for thee,

Oh, wea - - - - - - - ry prod-i-gal, come...............
Wea - ry prod-i - gal, come, wea - ry prod-i-gal, come.

No. 197. I'll Live for Him.

C. R. Dunbar.

1. My life, my love, I give to Thee, Thou Lamb of God who died for me;
2. I now believe Thou dost receive, For Thou hast died that I might live;
3. Oh, since Thou'st died on Cal-va-ry, To save my soul and make me free,

D. C. *I'll live for Him who died for me, How hap-py then my life shall be,*

D. C.

Oh, may I ev - er faith-ful be, My Sav-ior and my God!
And now hence forth I'll trust in Thee, My Sav-ior and my God!
I'll con - se - crate my life to Thee, My Sav-ior and my God!

I'll live for Him who died for me, My Sav-ior and my God!

By permission.

No. 198.   He Will Never Let Us Fall.

P. B.   P. BILHORN.

1. I came to Je-sus in   my   sin, Con-fess-ing   all   my   need;
2. With-out the knowledge of   His   word, I feared, I   could not stand;
3. I wept and trem-bled as   I   knelt Be-fore   the   lamb of God;
4. My time, my will I yield   to   Him, My bod - y   and   my all;

He free-ly par-doned, took me   in, And now His   blood I plead.
When some one whispered Christ the Lord, Will hold you   by His hand.
The Spir-it's pow'r I plain-ly felt, And cleans-ing thro' the blood.
He'll ev-er keep me pure with-in, And nev-er let me fall.

CHORUS.

He will nev-er, nev-er let us fall; He will nev-er,

nev-er let us fall; As we trust His pow'r each

day   and hour, He will nev-er, nev-er let us fall.

No. 199. Where is My Soul To-night?

Martha J. Lankton.

Wm. J. Kirkpatrick.

1. Oft have I heard a voice that said, In tones that were soft and low,
2. Oft have I heard a warn-ing voice, That urged me to fly from sin;
3. Oft have I heard a ten-der voice, When troubled and care-op-pressed,
4. Oft have I heard a grieved, sad voice, En-treat-ing me o'er and o'er;

"Thy Savior has loved, and loves thee yet, Then why wilt thou slight Him so?"
To o-pen the door I long have closed And welcome the Sav-ior in.
And then like a wea-ry child I sighed In Je-sus to find a rest.
And if I re-fuse to hear it now, Per-haps it will come no more.

CHORUS.

But where is my soul, where is my soul, Where is my soul to-night?
Last v. *O Sav-ior, I yield, Sav-ior, I yield, Take Thou my soul to-night;*

That voice pleads on, pleads pa-tient-ly on, But where is my soul to-night?
I now be-lieve, and glad-ly re-ceive Thy mes-sage of grace to-night.

No. 200. Is there any Reason, Sinner?

J. E. WOLFE.   P. BILHORN.

1. Is there an-y rea-son, sin-ner, Why you should re-ject the Lord?
2. Thou art un-der con-dem-na-tion, Thou art al-to-geth-er lost;
3. Oh, then list-en to the sto-ry, How the Christ of God came down,
4. Tar-ry then no long-er, sin-ner? Thou art hast'ning to the grave!

Can you think of an-y rea-son You should tram-ple on His Word?
Thou art in the arms of Sa-tan, And the prey of death's dark host;
To re-deem thee from thy bond-age, And to give to thee a crown;
Now re-pent! de-cide for Je-sus! For 'tis he a-lone can save.

Cres.

Al-ways hath He dealt in mer-cy, Show'ring bless-ings on thy path;
Thou art bound in chains of bond-age, And how drear is thine es-tate,
Why not heark-en to the Gos-pel, Tell-ing how thine aw-ful guilt
Turn not from the Ho-ly Spir-it, Who is say-ing, "Cease thy strife!"

Oh, what mad-ness, then, to ling-er, In the shad-ow of His wrath.
Soon to die with-out a Sav-ior; Oh, how sad will be thy fate!
On the cross was all a-toned for, When for thee His blood was spilt;
Why not yield at once to Je-sus, And have ev-er-last-ing life?

No. 201. Wondrous Love.

Mrs. M. Stockton.

Wm. G. Fisher. By per.

1. God loved the world of sin - ners lost And ru - ined by the fall:
2. E'en now by faith I claim Him mine, The ris - en Son of God;
3. Love brings the glo - rious full - ness in, And to His saints makes known
4. Be - liev - ing souls, re - joic - ing go; There shall to you be giv'n
5. Of vic - t'ry now o'er sa - tan's pow'r Let all the ran - somed sing,

Sal - va tion full, at high - est cost, He of - fers free to all.
Re - demp - tion by His death I find, And cleans - ing thro' the blood.
The bless - ed rest from in - bred sin, Thro' faith in Christ a - lone.
A glo - rious fore - taste here be - low, Of end - less life in heav'n.
And tri - umph in the dy - ing hour Thro' Christ the Lord our King.

CHORUS.

Oh, 'twas love, 'twas won - drous love! The love of God to me; It

brought my Sav - ior from a - bove, To die on Cal - va - ry.

No. 202. Help thy Brother.

Mrs. E. R. Charles. Arr. by Miss A. B.   J. H. Tenney.

1. Is thy cruse of com-fort fail-ing? To thy need-y broth-er give,
2. For the soul grows rich in giv-ing; All its treas-ures come with God;
3. Tho' the storm is fierce-ly beat-ing, Rise and face the chill-y blast;
4. Is thy heart all sad and emp-ty? Free-ly God its void will fill;

And throughout thy pil-grim jour-ney From God's boun-ty thou shalt live.
And when-e'er we help a broth-er, In the Mas-ter's steps we trod.
Help thy broth-er ere he per-ish! Soon the day-light will be past.
Come and drink, and give to oth-ers, This thy troub-led soul shall still.

He who gave His chil-dren man-na Will thy por-tion still re-new;
Art thou burdened, weak, and faint-ing, Dost thou sigh to be set free?
Art thou wound-ed in the con-flict? List, thy strick-en com-rade's moan;
Is thy gift a liv-ing pow-er? Trust-ing self, its strength sinks low;

Scant-y fare for one will oft-en Make a roy-al feast for two;
Help to lift thy broth-er's bur-den, God will bear both it and thee;
Give to him thy pre-cious oint-ment, And that balm will heal thine own;
It can on-ly live by lov-ing, And by serv-ing love will grow;

Help thy Brother. Concluded.

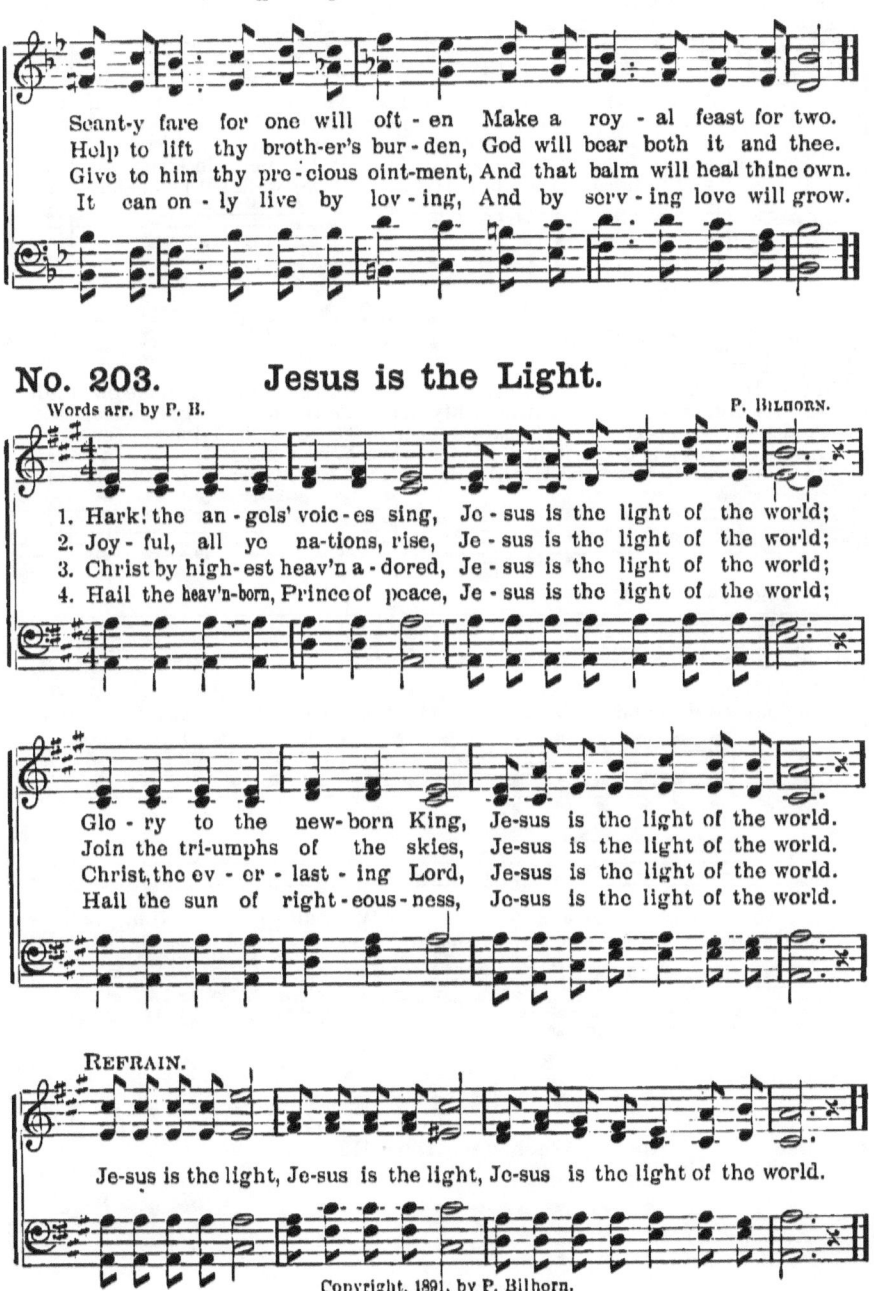

Scant-y fare for one will oft-en Make a roy-al feast for two.
Help to lift thy broth-er's bur-den, God will bear both it and thee.
Give to him thy pre-cious oint-ment, And that balm will heal thine own.
It can on-ly live by lov-ing, And by serv-ing love will grow.

No. 203.   Jesus is the Light.

Words arr. by P. B.   P. BILHORN.

1. Hark! the an-gels' voic-es sing, Je-sus is the light of the world;
2. Joy-ful, all ye na-tions, rise, Je-sus is the light of the world;
3. Christ by high-est heav'n a-dored, Je-sus is the light of the world;
4. Hail the heav'n-born, Prince of peace, Je-sus is the light of the world;

Glo-ry to the new-born King, Je-sus is the light of the world.
Join the tri-umphs of the skies, Je-sus is the light of the world.
Christ, the ev-er-last-ing Lord, Je-sus is the light of the world.
Hail the sun of right-eous-ness, Je-sus is the light of the world.

REFRAIN.

Je-sus is the light, Je-sus is the light, Je-sus is the light of the world.

No. 204. We Shall See Him.

Rev. Elisha A. Hoffman.   P. Bilhorn.

1. We are ab-sent here from the Lord we love, We shall see Him by and by;
2. Oh, the prom-ise sweet, we shall Je - sus meet, And be with Him where He is;
3. At the set of sun, when our work is done, He will stand at heav-en's door,
4. He will meet us there at the por - tals fair, Of the new Je - ru - sa - lem;
5. If we love the Lord and o - bey His word, If we walk with Je - sus here,

Share His bliss and love in the home a - bove, In the hap - py home on high.
In His like-ness come to our heav'nly home, To the home more fair than this.
And a wel-come give, and His saints receive, To be with Him ev - er-more.
And His loved and own will for - ev - er crown With a king - ly di - a - dem.
In His beau - ty dressed, with His like-ness blest, At His throne we shall ap - pear.

CHORUS.

We shall see Him, and be like Him, We shall see Him, by and by. We shall see Him, and be like Him.
We shall see Him, and be like Him, We shall see Him, and be like Him, We shall see Him, and be like Him, by and by, by and by. We shall see Him, and be like Him, we shall see Him, and be like Him,

We shall see Him in His glo-ry by and by.
by and by.

No. 205. Triumph By and By.

Dr. C. R. BLACKALL.

H. R. PALMER.

1. The prize is set be-fore us, To win His words im-plore us, The
2. We'll fol-low where He lead-eth, We'll pas-ture where He feedeth, We'll
3. Our home is bright a-bove us, No tri-als dark to move us, But

eye of God is o'er us, From on high(from on high):His lov-ing tones are calling,
yield to Him who pleadeth, From on high(from on high): Then naught from Him shall sever,
Je-sus dear to love us, There on high(there on high); We'll give Him best en-deav-or,

While sin is dark, ap-pall-ing, 'Tis Je-sus gently call-ing, He is nigh(He is nigh).
Our hope shall brighten ever, And faith shall fail us nev-er, He is nigh(He is nigh).
And praise His name forever; His precious ones can never, nev-er die (nev-er die).

CHORUS.

By and by we shall meet Him, By and by we shall greet Him, And with

1. Je-sus reign in glory, by and by. (by and by); 2. Jesus reign in glory by and by.

No. 206. Master, the Tempest is Raging.

M. A. BAKER.

H. R. PALMER.

1. Mas-ter, the tem-pest is rag-ing, The bil-lows are toss-ing high; The
2. Mas-ter, with an-guish of spir-it I bow in my grief to-day; The
3. Mas-ter, the ter-ror is o-ver, The el-e-ments sweet-ly rest; Earth's

sky is o'ershadowed with blackness, No shel-ter or help is nigh;
depths of my sad heart are trou-bled, Oh, wak-en and save, I pray!
sun in the calm lake is mir-rored, And heav-en's with-in my breast;

"Car-est Thou not that we per-ish?" How canst Thou lie a-sleep, When each
Tor-rents of sin and of an-guish Sweep o'er my sink-ing soul; And I
Lin-ger, O bless-ed Re-deem-er, Leave me a-lone no more; And with

mo-ment so mad-ly is threat'ning A grave in the an-gry deep?
per-ish! I per-ish! dear Mas-ter— Oh, hast-en, to take con-trol.
joy I shall make the blest har-bor, And rest on the bliss-ful shore.

Master, the Tempest is Raging. Concluded.

CHORUS.

p   *pp*

The winds and the waves shall o - bey Thy will, Peace, be still!

Peace, be still! peace, be still!

Whether the wrath of the storm-tossed sea, Or de-mons or men, or what-

Cres - - - - - - - *cen*

ev - er it be, No wa-ters can swal-low the ship where lies The Mas-ter of

- *do.* *ff*   *m*

o-cean, and earth, and skies, They all so sweet-ly o - bey Thy will, Peace be still!

p   *p*   *pp*

Peace, be still! They all so sweet-ly o - bey Thy will, Peace, peace, be still!

No. 207.   "'Tis Better Higher Up."

The following incident, abbreviated, which is often told by an Evangelist, suggested the hymn. An aged lady, once living in an upper story of an old building, was visited one day by a lady mission- ary, having in her company a well-dressed woman. As they were ascending the first flight of stairs, the wealthy person remarked; "Oh, my! how dark and dreary it is here!" "Never mind," answered the other, "'Tis better higher up." When they had reached and entered the top room, she again re- marked to the sick saint (whose life was ebbing away). "How can you live up here, and be contented in this dark, dreary, lonesome place?" The dying saint, pointing heavenward, with a smile, said; "'Tis better higher up."

Rev. G. W. Crofts.   P. Bilhorn.

1. This world is full of care, And bit-ter is life's cup
2. I've seen my hopes de-cay Like blos-soms in the Spring,
3. The storms of death have blown, But Christ, my bless-ed hope,
4. My flesh must fail, I know, And yet I can not grieve;
5. And in my home a-bove On joy di-vine I'll sup,

The cross is some-times hard to bear, "'Tis bet-ter high-er up."
My dear-est friends have passed a-way, Earth's treasures tak-en wing.
His ten-der love to me hath shown, "'Tis bet-ter high-er up."
The spir-it tells me I must go With Christ my Lord to live.
And rest in God's e-ter-nal love; "'Tis bet-ter high-er up."

CHORUS. *Faster.*

'Tis bet-ter high-er up, 'Tis bet-ter high-er up,

Where all is light, and peace, and joy, "'Tis bet-ter high-er up."

No. 208. Crown Him Lord of All.

1 All hail the power of Jesus' name!
Let angels prostrate fall;
Bring forth the royal diadem,
And crown Him Lord of all.

2 Crown Him, ye morning stars of light,
Who fixed this earthly ball;
Now hail the strength of Israel's might,
And crown Him Lord of all.

3 Ye chosen seed of Israel's race,
Ye ransomed from the fall,
Hail Him who saves you by His grace,
And crown Him Lord of all.

4 Sinners, whose love can ne'er forget
The wormwood and the gall;
Go, spread your trophies at His feet,
And crown Him Lord of all.

5 Let every kindred, every tribe,
On this terrestrial ball,
To Him all majesty ascribe,
And crown Him Lord of all.

6 O that with yonder sacred throng
We at His feet may fall!
We'll join the everlasting song,
And crown Him Lord of all.

No. 209. Just as I Am.

1 Just as I am, without one plea,
But that Thy blood was shed for me,
And that Thou bidd'st me come to Thee,
O Lamb of God, I come! I come!

2 Just as I am, and waiting not
To rid my soul of one dark blot,
To Thee, whose blood can cleanse each spot,
O Lamb of God, I come! I come!

3 Just as I am, though tossed about
With many a conflict, many a doubt,
Fightings within, and fears without,
O Lamb of God, I come! I come!

4 Just as I am—poor, wretched, blind;
Sight, riches, healing of the mind,
Yea, all I need, in Thee to find,
O Lamb of God, I come! I come!

5 Just as I am—Thou wilt receive,
Wilt welcome, pardon, cleanse, relieve;
Because Thy promise I believe,
O Lamb of God, I come! I come!

6 Just as I am—Thy love unknown
Hath broken every barrier down;
Now, to be Thine, yea, Thine alone,
O Lamb of God, I come! I come!

No. 210. Come, Every Soul.

1 Come, every soul by sin oppressed,
There's mercy with the Lord,
And He will surely give you rest,
By trusting in His word.

Cho.—Only trust Him, only trust Him,
Only trust Him now;
He will save you, He will save you,
He will save you now.

2 For Jesus shed His precious blood
Rich blessings to bestow;
Plunge now into the crimson tide
That washes white as snow.

Cho.—Come to Jesus, come to Jesus,
Come to Jesus now;
He will save you, He will save you,
He will save you now.

3 Yes, Jesus is the Truth, the Way,
That leads you into rest;
Believe in Him without delay,
And you are fully blest.

Cho.—Don't reject Him, don't reject Him,
Don't reject Him now;
He will save you, He will save you,
He will save you now.

4 O Jesus, blessed Jesus, dear,
I'm coming now to Thee,
Since Thou hast made the way so clear,
And full salvation free.

Cho.—I will trust Him, I will trust Him,
I will trust Him now;
He will save me, He will save me,
He will save me now.

5 Come, then, and join this holy band,
And on to glory go;
To dwell in that celestial land,
Where joys immortal flow.

No. 211. I Have a Savior.

1 I have a Savior, He's pleading in glory,
A dear, loving Savior, tho' earth friends be few;
And now He is watching in tenderness o'er me,
And, oh! that my Savior were your Savior too!

Cho.—For you I am praying,
For you I am praying,
For you I am praying,
I'm praying for you.

2 I have a Father: to me He has given
A hope for eternity, blessed and true;
And soon will He call me to meet Him in heaven,
But, oh! that He'd let me bring you with me too!

3 I have a peace: it is calm as a river—
A peace that the friends of the world never know;
My Savior alone is its Author and Giver,
And, oh! could I know it was given to you!

4 When Jesus has found you, tell others the story,
That my loving Savior is your Savior too;
Then pray that your Savior may bring them to glory,
And prayer will be answered—'twas answered for you!

No. 212. Praise God.

Arr. by P. Bilhorn.

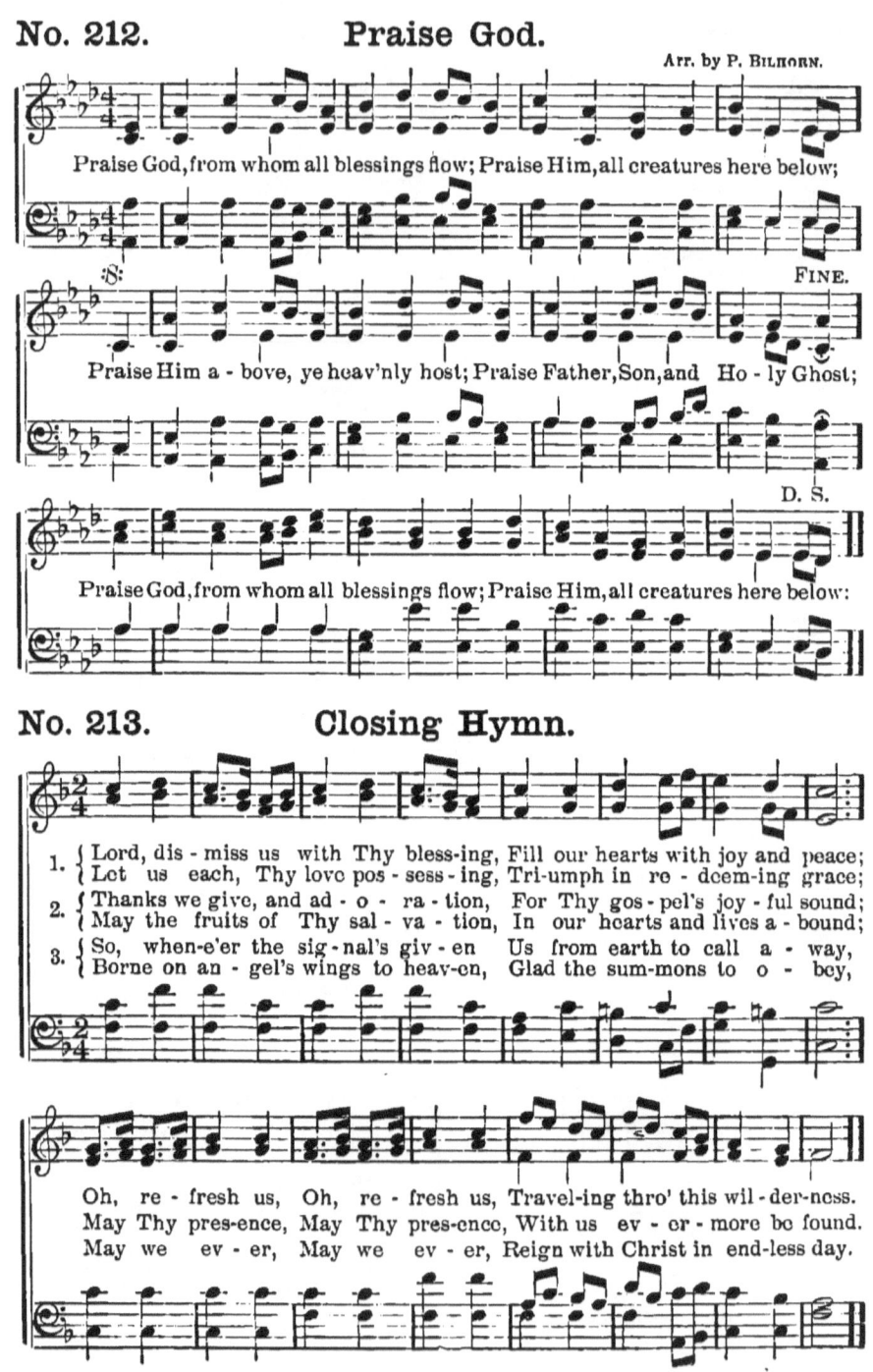

Praise God, from whom all blessings flow; Praise Him, all creatures here below;

Praise Him a - bove, ye heav'nly host; Praise Father, Son, and Ho - ly Ghost;

FINE.

D. S.

Praise God, from whom all blessings flow; Praise Him, all creatures here below:

No. 213. Closing Hymn.

1. { Lord, dis - miss us with Thy bless-ing, Fill our hearts with joy and peace;
   { Let us each, Thy love pos - sess-ing, Tri-umph in re - deem-ing grace;
2. { Thanks we give, and ad - o - ra - tion, For Thy gos - pel's joy - ful sound;
   { May the fruits of Thy sal - va - tion, In our hearts and lives a - bound;
3. { So, when-e'er the sig - nal's giv - en Us from earth to call a - way,
   { Borne on an - gel's wings to heav-en, Glad the sum-mons to o - bey,

Oh, re - fresh us, Oh, re - fresh us, Travel-ing thro' this wil - der-ness.
May Thy pres-ence, May Thy pres-ence, With us ev - er - more be found.
May we ev - er, May we ev - er, Reign with Christ in end-less day.

⤙« INDEX.»⤚

Titles in Roman. *First Lines in Italics.*